W9-APW-612

ALSO BY RACHEL CUSK

SECOND PLACE

SECOND PLACE

Rachel Cusk

FARRAR, STRAUS AND GIROUX

NEW YORK

Farrar, Straus and Giroux
120 Broadway, New York 10271

Copyright © 2021 by Rachel Cusk
All rights reserved
Printed in the United States of America
First edition, 2021

Library of Congress Cataloging-in-Publication Data
Names: Cusk, Rachel, 1967– author.
Title: Second place / Rachel Cusk.
Description: First edition. | New York : Farrar, Straus and Giroux,
    2021.
Identifiers: LCCN 2020053576 | ISBN 9780374279226 (hardcover)
Classification: LCC PR6053.U825 S43 2021 | DDC 823/.914—
    dc23
LC record available at https://lccn.loc.gov/2020053576

Our books may be purchased in bulk for promotional,
educational, or business use. Please contact your local bookseller
or the Macmillan Corporate and Premium Sales Department
at 1-800-221-7945, extension 5442, or by email at
MacmillanSpecialMarkets@macmillan.com.

www.fsgbooks.com
www.twitter.com/fsgbooks • www.facebook.com/fsgbooks

1   3   5   7   9   10   8   6   4   2

SECOND PLACE

I once told you, Jeffers, about the time I met the devil on a train leaving Paris, and about how after that meeting the evil that usually lies undisturbed beneath the surface of things rose up and disgorged itself over every part of life. It was like a contamination, Jeffers: it got into everything and turned it bad. I don't think I realised how many parts of life there were, until each one of them began to release its capacity for badness. I know you've always known about such things, and have written about them, even when others didn't want to hear and found it tiresome to dwell on what was wicked and wrong. Nonetheless you carried on, building a shelter for people to use when things went wrong for them too. And go wrong they always do!

Fear is a habit like any other, and habits kill what is essential in ourselves. I was left with a kind of blankness, Jeffers, from those years of being afraid. I kept on expecting things to jump out at me – I kept expecting to hear the same laughter of that devil I heard the day he pursued me up and down the train. It was the middle of the afternoon and very hot, and the carriages were crowded enough that

I thought I could get away from him merely by going and sitting somewhere else. But every time I moved my seat, a few minutes later there he'd be, sprawled across from me and laughing. What did he want with me, Jeffers? He was horrible in appearance, yellow and bloated with bloodshot bile-coloured eyes, and when he laughed he showed dirty teeth with one entirely black tooth right in the middle. He wore earrings and dandyish clothes that were soiled with the sweat that came pouring out of him. The more he sweated, the more he laughed! And he gabbled non-stop, in a language I couldn't recognise – but it was loud, and full of what sounded like curses. You couldn't exactly ignore it, and yet that was precisely what all the people in the carriages did. He had a girl with him, Jeffers, a shocking little creature, nothing more than a painted child who was barely clothed – she sat on his knee with parted lips and the soft gaze of a dumb animal while he fondled her, and nobody said or did a thing to stop him. Of all the people on that train, was it true that the one most likely to try was me? Perhaps he followed me up and down the carriages to tempt me into it. But it was not my own country: I was only passing through, going back to a home I thought of with secret dread, and it didn't seem up to me to stop him. It's so easy to think you don't matter all that much at the very moment when your moral duty as a self is most exposed. If I'd stood up to him, perhaps all the things that happened afterwards wouldn't have occurred. But for once I thought, let someone else do it! And that is how we lose control over our own destinies.

My husband Tony sometimes says to me that I underestimate my own power, and I wonder whether that makes living more hazardous for me than for other people, the way it's dangerous for those who lack the ability to feel pain. I've often thought that there are certain characters who can't or won't learn the lesson of life, and that they live among us as either a nuisance or a gift. What they cause can be called trouble or it can be called change – but the point is, though they may not mean to or want to, they make it happen. They're always stirring things up and objecting and upsetting the status quo; they won't just leave things be. They themselves are neither bad nor good – that's the important thing about them – but they know good from bad when they see it. Is this how the bad and the good continue to flourish alongside each other in our world, Jeffers, because certain people won't let either one get the upper hand? That day on the train, I decided to pretend not to be one of them. Life looked so much easier all of a sudden, over there behind the books and newspapers people were holding up in front of their faces to hide the devil from their sight!

What is certain is that afterwards many changes occurred, and I had to use all my strength and my belief in right and my capacity for pain to survive them, so that I nearly died from it – and after that, I was no longer a nuisance to anyone. Even my mother decided she liked me for a while. Eventually I found Tony and he helped me recover, and when he gave me the life of peace and gentleness here on the marsh, what did I do but find fault with the beauty and the peace and try to stir them up! You know about that story, Jeffers, because I've written it down elsewhere – I mention it only to help you see how it connects to what

I want to tell you about now. It seemed to me that all this beauty was no good if it had no immunity: if I could harm it, then anyone could. Whatever power it is that I have, it's nothing compared to the power of stupidity. That was and remains my reasoning, even though I could have taken the opportunity to live an idyll here of easeful impotence. Homer says it in *The Iliad*, when he mentions the pleasant homes and occupations of the men cut down in battle, not forgetting their fancy battledress and their hand-tooled chariots and armour. All that sweet cultivating and building, all that possession, to be chopped apart with a sword, stamped out in the seconds it takes to stamp on an ant.

I'd like to go with you, Jeffers, back to the morning in Paris before I boarded the train that held the bloated, yellow-eyed devil: I'd like to make you see it. You are a moralist, and it will take a moralist to understand how it was that one of the fires that started that day was allowed to keep on smouldering over the years, how its core stayed alive unnoticed and secretly fed itself, until the time when my circumstances were finally replenished and it caught alight on the new things and blazed again into life. That fire was laid in Paris, in the early morning, where a seducing dawn lay over the pale forms of the Île de la Cité and the air was held in the absolute stillness that presages a beautiful day. The sky got bluer and more blue and the green fresh banks of foliage were motionless in the warmth, and the blocks of light and shadow that bisected the streets were like the eternal primordial shapes that lie on the faces of mountain ranges and seem to come

6

from inside them. The city was quiet and mostly empty of humans, so that it felt as though it were itself more than human and could only reveal it when there was no one to see. I had lain awake all the short hot summer night in my hotel bed and so when I saw dawn between the curtains I had got up and gone down to walk beside the river. It seems presumptuous, Jeffers, not to mention meaningless, to describe my experience in this way, as if it had the slightest bit of significance. Doubtless someone else is walking beside that same stretch of river at this minute, likewise committing the sin of believing that things happen for a reason, and that that reason is herself! But I need to give you my state of mind on that morning, the exalted sense of possibility I felt, to make you understand what came out of it.

I had spent the evening in the company of a famous writer, who was actually nothing more significant than a very lucky man. I met him at an art gallery opening, from which he took sufficient pains to extricate me that my vanity was gratified. I didn't get sexual attention very often in those years, though I was young, and I suppose good-looking enough. The trouble was, I had the dumb loyalty of a dog. This writer was of course an insufferable egotist, as well as a liar, and not even a very believable one; and I, alone in Paris for the night, with my disapproving husband and child waiting back at home, was so thirsty for love I would drink, it seemed, from any source. Truly, Jeffers, I was a dog – there was such a heavy weight inside me, I could only writhe senselessly like an animal in pain. It pinned me down in the depths, where I thrashed and struggled to get free and swim to the brilliant surface of life – at least, that's how it looked from below. In the company of the egotist, tramping from bar to bar in the Paris night, I intimated for the first time the possibility of destruction, the destruction of what I had built; not, I assure you, for his sake, but for the possibility he embodied – which had never once oc-curred to me until that night – of violent change. The egotist, permanently drunk on his own importance, sliding breath mints between his dry lips when he thought I wouldn't no-tice and talking about himself non-stop: he didn't actually fool me, though I admit I wanted him to. He gave me plenty of rope to hang him with, but of course I didn't hang him – I played along, half believing it myself, which was more of the luck he'd evidently had all his life. We said goodbye at two in the morning at the entrance to the hotel, where he visibly – to the point of unchivalrousness – decided I wasn't worth whatever risk to his status quo our spending the night together would have represented. And I went to bed and hugged the memory of his attention until the roof seemed to lift off the hotel and the walls to fall away and the huge starry darkness to embrace me with the implica-tions of what I felt.

Why do we live so painfully in our fictions? Why do we suffer so, from the things we ourselves have invented? Do you understand it, Jeffers? I have wanted to be free my whole life and I haven't managed to liberate my smallest toe. I believe Tony is free, and his freedom doesn't look like much. He gets on his blue tractor to mow the tall grass that has to be cut back for spring and I watch him calmly going up and down in his big floppy hat under the sky, back and forth in the noise of the engine. All around him the cherry trees are welling up, the little nubs on their branches straining to burst into blossom for him, and the skylark shoots into the sky as he passes and hangs there singing and twirling like an acrobat. Meanwhile, I just sit staring straight in front of me with nothing to do. That's all I've managed as far as freedom is concerned, to get rid of the people and the things I don't like. After that, there isn't all that much left! When Tony's been working on the land I rouse myself to cook for him, and go out to pick herbs from the garden and to look in the shed for potatoes. At that time of year – the spring – the potatoes we store in the shed start to sprout, even though we keep them in complete darkness. They throw out these white fleshy arms because they know it's spring, and sometimes I'll look at one and realise a potato knows more than most people do.

The morning after that night in Paris, when I got up and walked beside the river, my body barely felt the ground: the green glittering water, and the worn slanted stone walls of palest beige, and the early sun shining on them and on me as I moved through them, made such a buoyant element that I became weightless. I wonder whether that is what it feels like to be loved – by which I mean the important love, the one you receive before you know strictly speaking that you exist. My safety in that moment felt limitless. What was it, I wonder, that I saw to make me feel that way, when in reality I was any-thing but safe? When in fact I had glimpsed the germ of a possibility that was soon to grow and rage like a cancer through my life, consuming years, consuming substance; when a few hours later I would be sitting face-to-face with the devil himself?

I must have wandered along for quite some time, because when I came back up to the street the shops were open and there were people and cars moving around in the sun. I was hungry, and so I started to pay attention to the shopfronts, looking for somewhere I could buy something to eat. I'm not good in that situation, Jeffers: I find it difficult to answer my own needs. The sight of other people getting what they want, jostling and demanding things, makes me decide I would rather go without. I hold back, embarrassed by need – my own and other people's. This sounds like a ridiculous quality, and I've always known I would be the first to be trampled underfoot in a crisis, though I've noticed that children are also like this and find the needs of their particular body embarrassing. When I say this to Tony, that I would be the first to go under because I wouldn't fight for my share, he laughs and says he doesn't think so. So much for self-knowledge, Jeffers!

Whatever the truth is, there weren't many people about that morning in Paris, and the streets where I was walking, which were somewhere near the Rue du Bac, were entirely devoid of things to eat in the first place. Instead the shops were full of exotic fabrics and antiques and colonial-era curios costing several weeks of an ordinary person's wages, and of a particular fragrance which was the fragrance, I suppose, of money, and I looked in the windows as I passed, as though I were considering making a purchase of a large carved-wood African head at that early hour of the morning. The streets were perfect chasms of light and shade and I made sure to stay in the sun, walking without any other purpose or direction. Presently, ahead of me, I saw a sign that had been set out on the pavement, and on that sign was an image. The image, Jeffers, was of a painting by L, and it was part of an advertisement for an exhibition of his work at a gallery nearby. Even from a distance I recognised something about it, though I still can't say quite what it was, because though I had vaguely heard of L, I had no real idea when or how I had heard of him, nor of who he was or what he painted. Nonetheless he spoke to me: he addressed me there on that Paris street, and I followed the signs one after another until I arrived at the gallery and walked straight in through the open door.

You will want to know, Jeffers, which of his paintings they'd chosen for the advertisement and why it affected me in that way. There is no particular reason, on the surface, why L's work should summon a woman like me, or perhaps any woman – but least of all, surely, a young mother on the brink of rebellion whose impossible yearnings, moreover, are crystallised in reverse by the aura of absolute freedom his paintings emanate, a freedom elementally and unrepentingly male down to the last brushstroke. It's a question that begs an answer, and yet there is no clear and satisfying answer, except to say that this aura of male freedom belongs likewise to most representations of the world and of our human experience within it, and that as women we grow accustomed to translating it into something we ourselves can recognise. We get our dictionaries and we puzzle it out, and avoid some of the parts we can't make sense of or understand, and some others we know we're not entitled to, and voilà!, we participate. It's a case of borrowed finery, and sometimes of downright impersonation; and having never felt all that womanly in the first place, I believe the habit of impersonation has gone deeper in me than most, to the extent that some aspects of me do seem in fact to be male. The fact is that I received the clear message from the very beginning that everything would have been better – would have been right, would have been how it ought to be – had I been a boy. Yet I never found any use for that male part, as L went on to show me later, in the time I will tell you about.

The painting, by the way, was a self-portrait, one of L's arresting portraits where he shows himself at about the distance you might keep between yourself and a stranger. He looks almost surprised to see himself: he gives that stranger a glance that is as objective and compassionless as any glance in the street. He is wearing an ordinary kind of plaid shirt and his hair is brushed back and parted, and despite the coldness of the act of perception – which is a cosmic coldness and loneliness, Jeffers – the rendering of those details, of the buttoned-up shirt and the brushed hair and the plain features unanimated by recognition, is the most human and loving thing in the world. Looking at it, the emotion I felt was pity, pity for myself and for all of us: the kind of wordless pity a mother might feel for her mortal child, who nonetheless she brushes and dresses so tenderly. It gave, you might say, the final touch to my strange, exalted state – I felt myself falling out of the frame I had lived in for years, the frame of human implication in a particular set of circumstances. From that moment, I ceased to be immersed in the story of my own life and became distinct from it. I had read my Freud often enough, and could have learned from there how silly it all was, but it took L's painting to make me really *see* it. I saw, in other words, that I was alone, and saw the gift and the burden of that state, which had never truly been revealed to me before.

You know, Jeffers, that I am interested in the existence of things before our knowledge of them – partly because I have trouble believing that they *do* exist! If you have always been criticised, from before you can remember, it becomes more or less impossible to locate yourself in the time or space before the criticism was made: to believe, in other words, that you yourself exist. The criticism is more real than you are: it seems, in fact, to have created you. I believe a lot of people walk around with this problem in their heads, and it leads to all kinds of trouble – in my case, it led to my body and my mind getting divorced from each other right at the start, when I was only a few years old. But my point is that there's something that paintings and other created objects can do to give you some relief. They give you a location, a place to be, when the rest of the time the space has been taken up because the criticism got there first. I don't include things created out of words, though: at least for me they don't have the same effect, because they have to pass through my mind to get to me. My appreciation of words has to be mental. Can you forgive me for that, Jeffers?

There wasn't another soul in the gallery that early in the morning, and the sun came through the big windows and made bright pools on the floor in the silence, and I stepped around as joyfully as a faun in a forest on the first day of creation. It was what they call a 'major retrospective,' which appears to mean you're finally important enough to be dead – even though L was barely forty-five then. There were at least four big rooms, but I ate them up, one after the other. Each time I stepped up to a frame – from the smallest sketch to the biggest of the landscape works – I got the same sensation, to the point where I thought it was impossible I'd get it again. But I did: over and over, as I faced the image, the sensation came. What was it? It was a feeling, Jeffers, but it was also a phrase. It will seem contradictory, after what I've just said about words, that words should accompany the sensation so definitively. But I didn't find those words. The paintings found them, somewhere inside me. I don't know who they belonged to, or even who spoke them – just that they were spoken.

A lot of the paintings were of women, and of one woman in particular, and my feelings about those were more recognisable, though even then somehow painless and disembodied. There was a small charcoal sketch of a woman asleep in bed, her dark head a mere smudge of oblivion in the tousled bedclothes. I admit a kind of silent bitter weeping did come from my heart at this record of passion, which seemed to define everything I hadn't known in my life, and I wondered if I ever would. In many of the larger portraits, L paints a dark-haired, quite fleshy woman – often he is in the painting with her – and I wondered whether this smudge in the bed, almost effaced by desire, was the same person. In the portraits she usually wears some kind of mask or disguise; sometimes she seems to love him, at others merely to be tolerating him. But his desire, when it comes, extinguishes her.

It was in the landscapes, though, that I heard the phrase the loudest, and it was these same images that stayed smouldering in my mind over the years, until the time came that I want to tell you about, Jeffers, when fire broke out again all around me. The religiousness of L's landscapes! If human existence can be a religion, that is. When he paints a landscape, he is remembering looking at it. That's the best I can do to describe the landscapes, or describe how I saw them and the way they made me feel. You would doubtless do far better. But the point is for you to understand how it was that the idea of L and his landscapes recurred all those years later and in another place, when I was living on the marsh with Tony and thinking quite differently. I realise now that I fell in love with Tony's marsh because it had precisely that same quality, the quality of something remembered, that shares and is inextricable from the moment of being. I could never capture it, and I don't know why I needed it to be captured at all, but that is as good an example of human determinism as we're likely to lay our hands on for now!

15

You will be wondering, Jeffers, what the phrase was that came out of L's paintings and spoke itself so clearly to me. It was: *I am here.* I won't say what I think the words mean, or who they refer to, because that would be to try to stop them living.

One day I wrote to L, inviting him to come to the marsh:

Dear L

Richard C gave me your details – I think we are both friends of his. I first came to know your work fifteen years ago, when it picked me up off the street and put me on the path to a different understanding of life. I mean that quite literally! These days I and my husband Tony live in a place of great but subtle beauty, where artists often seem to find the will or the energy or just the opportunity to work. I would like you to come here, to see what it looks like through your eyes. Our landscape is one of those conundrums people are drawn to, and end up missing the point of entirely. It is full of desolation and solace and mystery, and it hasn't yet told its secret to anyone. Twice a day the sea rises over the marsh and fills its creeks and crevices and bears away – or so I like to think of it – the evidence of its thoughts. I have walked on the marsh every day for these past years and it's never looked like the same place twice. They're always trying to paint it, of course, but what they end up painting is the contents of their own mind – they try to find drama or a story or a point of exception in it, when those things can only ever be incidental to its character. I think of the marsh as the vast woolly breast of some sleeping god or animal, whose motion is the deep, slow motion of somnambulant breathing. Those are just my opinions, but they make me bold enough to suspect that you might share them and that there is something here for you – and perhaps only for you.

We live simply and comfortably, and have a second place where people can stay and be quite alone if they want to be. We've had a number of guests here to do their own kind of work, one after another. They stay sometimes for days and sometimes for months. We don't keep a calendar and so far haven't seemed to need one – it all goes quite naturally. I repeat, you can be entirely alone if you wish to be. The summer is the best time and we have more visitors asking to come then. If you're at all interested in coming I can write again with more details of where we are, how we live, how to get here, etc. We are quite remote, though there is a small town a few miles away where you can find amenities if you

need them. People often say this is one of the
last places.

M

He replied, Jeffers, almost straight away, which came
as somewhat of a surprise. It made me wonder who else
I could summon up, simply by sitting down and directing
my will at them!

M

I got your note, and read it on the terrace of that
new restaurant in Malibu, shielding my eyes from
a bloodletting of a sunset that brought hellfire and
brimstone to mind. I'm in LA to hang my new show,
which opens in a couple of weeks. The pollution
is obscene. Your woolly marsh sounded nice by
comparison.

I haven't seen Richard C in years. I don't know
what he's doing now.

As it happens I'm alone, and free to try something
different. I'd like to try something. Perhaps what
you're suggesting is it. I wonder what it was you saw
that took you off the street.

Give me the details, anyhow. The place you
describe sounds isolated, but I've never yet found
anywhere I can be freer and more alone than New
York. Are there really no people, or does that small
town you mention harbour a cluster of arty types?

Let me know, anyhow.

L

ps: My gallerist says she's been somewhere that might be where you are. Is that possible? From how you described it, it didn't sound like somewhere she would go.

I wrote back, telling him more about Tony and me and about the life here and what he could expect of us, and trying to describe what the second place was like. I made sure not to exaggerate, Jeffers: Tony has taught me that my habit of wanting to please people by saying that things are better than they are just creates disappointment, mine more than anyone else's. It's a form of control, as so much of generosity is.

We built the second place when Tony bought a parcel of wasteland that bordered our land, to prevent it from being misused. The rules here about development are strict, but of course people find all kinds of ways to get around them. The most usual one is to plant trees in order to cut them down again for money, pale and sapless trees that grow fast and straight up in rows like soldiers and then are quickly felled like soldiers too, so that what's left is a shorn mess of amputated stumps. We didn't want those poor soldiers marching past our windows to their deaths day and night! So we bought it, intending to turn it over to nature, more or less, but once we'd started clearing away all the brambles and fallen trees we came upon a whole different story. Tony has a group of men he knows who all help one another when there's physical work to be done. Some of those bramble clumps were twenty feet high, Jeffers, and they scratched the men to death trying to defend themselves, but when they were cut away all sorts of things were hidden underneath them. We found a beautiful half-rotten clinker-built sailboat, and two old classic cars, and then finally an entire cottage buried beneath a mountain of ivy! It was the integuments of a life we uncovered, complete with a lovelier view of the marsh than our own. I have often wondered about the person who lived that life that had been so deeply forgotten it had been allowed, literally, to rot back into the earth. The cars were in profound and interesting stages of decay and we let them be, and mowed the grass around them so that they became objects of display; and likewise the boat, which stood at the top of an incline with its prow lifted toward the sea. I found the boat a little melancholy, since it always seemed to be calling to someone or something out of reach; but the cars continued to collapse majestically over time, as though bent on discovering a truth of their own. The cottage was quite sordid and quite sad, and we quickly realised it would have to be done over to rid it of that awful human type of sadness. The inside was entirely blackened by fire, and the men had the theory that therein was written the fate of the previous incumbent. So they took the whole thing down and built it back up again by hand, with Tony giving the directions.

You and Tony have never met, Jeffers, but I believe you would get along: he's very practical, as you yourself are, and not bourgeois, and not at all neglectful in the sense that the very souls of most bourgeois men are neglect-ful. He doesn't show the weakness of neglect, and nor does he need to neglect something in order to have power over it. He does have a number of Certainties, though, which come from his particular knowledge and position and which can be very useful and reassuring until you find yourself opposing one of them! I have never met an-other human being who is so little burdened by shame as Tony and so little inclined to make others feel ashamed of themselves. He doesn't comment and he doesn't criticise and this puts him in an ocean of silence compared to most people. Sometimes his silence makes me feel invisible, not to him but to myself, because as I've told you I've been criticised all my life: it's how I've come to know that I'm there. Yet because I am one of his Certainties, he finds it difficult to believe that I could doubt my own existence. 'You are asking me to criticise you,' he will sometimes say at the end of one or other of my outbursts. And that's all he'll say!

I'm telling you all this, Jeffers, because it has to do with the building of the second place and with what we de-cided to use it for, which was as a home for the things that weren't already here – the higher things, or so I thought them, that I had come to know and care about one way or another in my life. I don't mean that we envisaged starting some kind of community or utopia. It was simply that Tony understood I had interests of my own, and that just because he was satisfied with our life on the marsh it didn't automatically follow that I would be too. I needed some degree of communication, however small, with the notions of art and with the people who abide by those no-tions. And those people did come, and they did commu-nicate, though they always seemed to end up liking Tony more than they liked me!

When people marry young, Jeffers, everything grows out of the shared root of their youth and it becomes im-possible to tell which part is you and which the other person. So if you attempt to sever yourselves from one another it becomes a severance all the way from the roots to the furthest ends of the branches, a gory mess of a pro-cess that seems to leave you half of what you were before. But when you make a marriage later it is more like the meeting of two distinctly formed things, a kind of bump-ing into one another, the way whole landmasses bumped into one another and fused over geological time, leaving great dramatic seams of mountain ranges as the evidence of their fusing. It is less of an organic process and more of a spatial event, an external manifestation. People could live in and around Tony and me in a way they could never have entered and inhabited the dark core – whether living or dead – of an original marriage. Our relationship had plenty of openness, but it posed certain difficulties too, natural challenges that had to be surmounted: bridges had to be built and tunnels bored, to get across to one another out of what was pre-formed. The second place was one such bridge, and Tony's silence ran undisrupted beneath it like a river.

It stands across a gentle slope up from the main house, separated by a glade of trees through which the sun rises into our windows every morning; and the sun sets, through those same trees, in the evenings into the windows of the second place. Those windows go from the floor to the ceiling, so that the huge horizontal bar of the marsh and its drama – its sweeping passages of colour and light, the brewing of its distant storms, the great drifts of seabirds that float or settle over its pelt in white flecks, the sea that sometimes lies roaring at the very furthest line of the horizon in a boiling white foam and sometimes advances gleaming and silent until it has covered everything in a glassy sheet of water – seem to be right there in the room with you.

The windows were one of Tony's Certainties, and I disagreed with him and stood against him over them from the beginning, because I believe a house ought first and foremost to be cosy and to allow you to forget the outside when you're in it. The lack of privacy was troubling to me, especially at night when the lights were on and whoever was in there could forget that they could be seen as clear as day. I have a great fear of seeing people when they don't know they're being observed, and finding out things about them I'd be happier not knowing! But for Tony a view has a kind of spiritual significance, not as something you describe or talk about but as something you live in correspondence with, so that it looks back at you and incorporates itself in everything you do. I watch him pause when he's cutting wood or digging over the vegetables and lift his eyes to the marsh for a while, and then go back to what he's doing; and so we eat the marsh along with our vegetables, and warm ourselves with it in our fires in the evening.

Tony wouldn't hear me about the windows, and even went so far as to act as though he *couldn't* hear me, and afterwards, whenever I brought the subject up and talked about how much trouble they caused, he would listen to me in silence and then say, 'I like them.' I suppose that was his way of admitting he might have been wrong. The very first time we had a visitor, a musician who was trying to record and replicate patterns of birdsong and who turned the whole place into a studio full of big black boxes and fantastic dashboards with dials and blinking lights, I went across through the trees to bring some post that had arrived for him, and there he was standing stark naked at the stove, frying some eggs! I would have crept away, except that he saw me through the windows the same way I had seen him, and had to come to the door and take his post, still without a stitch on, because he had obviously decided it was better to pretend that nothing out of the ordinary had happened.

Or perhaps nothing *had* happened, Jeffers – perhaps the world is full of people like Tony and this man, who think there's nothing to be worried about in seeing and being seen, with clothes or without them!

I was allowed after that episode to hang up some curtains, and I was very proud of those beautiful curtains made of a thick pale linen, even though I knew they caused Tony to have a pain in his eyes every time he saw them. The floors were made of wide chestnut planks that the men had planed and sanded themselves and the walls were rough white lime-plaster, and all the cupboards and shelves were made of the same chestnut wood, so that the whole place felt very human and natural, all shapely and textured and sweet-smelling, and not at all clinical and squared off in the way that some new places feel. We made one big room with the stove and the fire and some comfortable chairs, and a long wooden table for eating and working at; and then another smaller room for sleeping, and a bathroom with a nice old cast-iron bath in it that I had found in a junk shop. It was all so fresh and lovely, I was ready to move in there myself. When it was finished, Tony said:

'Justine will think we made this place for her.'

Well, I can't say it hadn't occurred to me to wonder what my daughter would think of the work we'd done, but it certainly hadn't crossed my mind that she might believe it had been done in her honour! As soon as Tony said it, though, I knew it was true, and I immediately felt guilty, while at the same time determined not to have something stolen from me. These two feelings, always coming in a pair, the better to incapacitate and handcuff me – I have been troubled by them right from the beginning, when Justine arrived on this earth and seemed to want to stand in the same spot that I stood in, only I was there first. I could never reconcile myself to the fact that just as you've recovered from your own childhood, and finally crawled out of the pit of it and felt the sun on your face for the first time, you have to give up that place in the sun to a baby you're determined won't suffer the way you did, and crawl back down into another pit of self-sacrifice to make sure she doesn't! At that time

Justine had just finished college and gone off to Berlin to work for an organisation there, but she often came back to visit seeming faintly unsettled, with a transitory air of immediate need, like a person in a busy station looking around for somewhere to sit while they wait for their train. No matter how nice a seat I found for her, she always preferred the look of the one I was sitting in. I wondered whether we ought to offer the second place to her straight away and get it over with, but as it happened she fell in love with a man called Kurt and didn't come back at all that summer, and our new life of having visitors to the marsh began.

I didn't, obviously, go into all this ancient history in my letter to L, only as much of it as I thought he needed to know. There were a few weeks of silence while life went on as usual, and then all at once he wrote saying he was coming, and coming the very next month! Fortunately we didn't happen to have any visitors just then, and so Tony and I flew around the second place, repainting the walls and re-waxing the floors and cleaning the windows with newspaper and vinegar until they shone. The first blossoms had just burst out of the cherry trees after the winter and the glade was frothing with the lovely pink and white flowers, and we cut a few branches and arranged them in big earthenware jars and even laid a fire in the grate. My arms ached from cleaning those windows and we fell into bed exhausted in the evenings, having barely been able to cook a meal for ourselves.

Then L wrote again:

M

After all I decided to go somewhere else. Someone
I know has an island he says I can use. It's meant to
be sort of a paradise. So I'm going to go and try
being Robinson Crusoe for a while. It's a pity not to
be calling in at your marsh. I keep meeting people
who know you, and they say you're okay.

L

Well, we accepted it, Jeffers, though I won't say I forgot
about it – the summer went on to be the hottest and most
glorious summer we'd had in years, and we lit bonfires at
night and slept outside underneath skies throbbing with
stars, and swam in the tidal creeks, and I kept imagining
how it would have been if L had been there with us and
how he would have looked at it. A writer came to stay in
the second place instead of L, and we barely saw him.
He spent all day indoors with the curtains closed, even
in the hottest weather – I believe he was asleep! But I did
often think about L on his island, and about what kind of
paradise it was, and even though our own place was more
or less paradisiacal that summer I made myself jealous by
thinking about it. It was as if some breeze kept wafting toward me, bearing a tormenting scent of freedom – and that
same torment suddenly seemed to have bothered and
pursued me for too much of my life. I felt I had dismantled
everything and run this way and that trying to get at it, the
way someone with a bee sting might tear at their clothes
and run around making their agony visible to people who
don't know what's wrong. I kept trying to make Tony talk

to me about it – I felt a burning need to speak, to analyse, to get these feelings out of me into the open where I could see them and walk around them. One night, when Tony and I were going to bed, I flew at him in a rage and said all kinds of terrible things, about how lonely and washed up I felt, about how he never gave me any real attention of the kind that makes a woman feel like a woman and just expected me to sort of give birth to myself all the time, like Venus out of a seashell. As if I knew anything about what makes a woman feel like a woman! In the end I flounced off to sleep on the couch downstairs, and I lay there and thought about what I'd said and about how Tony never does anything to hurt or control me, and in the end I ran back upstairs and jumped into bed with him and said:

'Oh Tony, I'm sorry to have said such terrible things. I know how good you are to me and I don't want ever to hurt you. It's just that sometimes I need to talk in order to feel real, and I wish you would talk to me.'

He was silent, lying on his back in the darkness and staring up at the ceiling. Then he said:

'I feel like my heart is talking to you all the time.'

So there you have it, Jeffers! Truly I think Tony believes that talk and gossip are a poison, and this is one of the reasons the people who come here like him so much, because he acts as a kind of antidote to their habit of poisoning themselves and others and makes them feel much healthier. But for me there *is* a healthy kind of talking, though it's rare – the kind of talking through which people create themselves by giving themselves utterance. I often had this kind of talk with the artists and other people who came to the marsh, though they were quite capable of the poisonous talk too, and did talk like that a lot of the time. There were enough instances of being in sympathy with one another, of transcending our own selves and mingling through language, for me not to mind it.

In the autumn I was surprised to get another letter from L:

M

So okay, paradise isn't all it's cracked up to be. I got tired of all the sand. Also I got an infected cut and had to be rescued by a seaplane and flown to hospital. I spent six weeks in the hospital, time wasted. Life passed outside the windows. Now I'm going to Rio, for my show there. I've never been to that part of the world but it sounds like it could be a ball. I might stay the winter.

L

Just as I'd settled down again, now I had to walk around with Rio de Janeiro in my head day and night, all hot and noisy and carnal and full of licentious fun! The rain had started to fall and the trees grew bare and the winds of winter moaned across the marsh. Sometimes I would get out the catalogue of L's work and look at the images and feel the sensation they always gave me. And of course there were a million other strands to life and things that happened and took up our thoughts and feelings, but it is my dealings with L that concern me here and that I want to make you see, Jeffers. I don't want to give the impression that I thought about him more than I did. The thoughts about him – which were really about his work – were cyclical, like a consummation. They consummated my solitary self, and supplied it with a kind of continuity.

All the same, I more or less gave up the idea of L ever coming to where I was and looking at it through his own eyes, which would have taken that consummation to a point of finality and given me – or so I believed – a version of the freedom I had wanted my whole life. He wrote to me a couple of times over the winter, telling me about all the things he was doing in Rio, and once even inviting me to go over there myself! But I had no intention of going to Rio, nor of going anywhere, and the letter annoyed me because it trivialised me and also because its tone forced me to conceal it from Tony. I think what it meant was that he was, somehow, afraid of me, and his treating me as he presumably treated other women was a way of getting himself back on firm ground.

The events of that winter are familiar to everyone, and so I needn't go over them, except to say that we felt their impact far less than most people did. We had already simplified our existence, but for others that process of simplification was brutal and agonising. The only thing that really irked me was that it was no longer so easy to go anywhere – not that we ever went anywhere in any case! But I felt the loss of that freedom nonetheless. You know, Jeffers, that I have no particular country and am not really a citizen of any place, so there was a feeling of imprisonment that came with knowing I had to stay where I was. Also, it made it harder for people to come to see us, but by that time Justine had been forced to return from Berlin, and had brought Kurt with her, and so we gave them the second place to live in, as had been ordained at the very beginning.

In the spring I received a letter.

M

Well, hasn't everything gone completely crazy.
Maybe not for you. But I've gone tits-up, as my
English friend likes to put it. All the value wiped off
of everything like a layer of scum. I lost my house,
and also my place in the country. I never felt like
they belonged to me in any case. The other day
I heard someone in the street say of this global
pandemonium that it will completely alter the
character of Brooklyn. Ha ha!

Do you still have a space? I think I can get to you.
I know a way. Do I need any money to be there?

L

Because this is partly a story of will, and of the consequences of exerting it, you will notice, Jeffers, that everything I determined to happen happened, but not as I wanted it! This is the difference, I suppose, between an artist and an ordinary person: the artist can create outside himself the perfect replica of his own intentions. The rest of us just create a mess, or something hopelessly wooden, no matter how brilliantly we imagined it. That's not to say that we don't all of us have some compartment in which we too are able to achieve ourselves instinctively, to leap without looking, but the bringing of things into permanent existence is an achievement of a different order. The closest most people come to it is in having a child. And nowhere are our mistakes and limitations more plainly written than there!

I sat down with Justine and Kurt and explained to them what had happened, and that they were going to have to move into the main house with us after all – and of course Justine wanted to know why L couldn't be in the house with us instead. Well, I didn't entirely know why he couldn't, just that the thought of it – of me and Tony and L all living at close quarters – made me want to shrivel up, and that the prospect of trying to explain it to Justine was almost as bad. It made me feel old, older than the most ancient monument, which is how children make you feel when you still presume to produce an original feeling of your own now and then. Language entirely fails me at such moments, the parental language that one way or another I've neglected to keep up and maintain, so that it's like a rusty engine that won't start when you need it. I didn't want to be anyone's parent in that minute!

Kurt, unexpectedly, came to my rescue. I hadn't had much to do with him up to that point, reasoning that it was none of my business who or what he was, though he had a way of making it obvious that he was thinking something very different from what he was saying when he talked to you that I wasn't sure I liked all that much. It seemed to me that if that was what you were doing, you shouldn't be so proud of its being obvious. He was quite thin and delicate, and a very elegant dresser, and there was something bird-like in his long fragile neck with the beaky face above it and in his fine plumage. He turned to Justine and cocked his head in that birdlike way and said:

'But Justine, they can't have a complete stranger sharing their house.'

It was noble of him, Jeffers, considering that he was more or less a complete stranger himself, and I was pleased to have my point of view encapsulated in that way – it made me feel quite sane after all. And Justine, as good as gold, thought about it for a minute and then agreed that no, she supposed we couldn't, so that Kurt's well-brought-up-ness even had the unexpected effect of bringing out good manners in my own child – I was quite impressed. If only he would get rid of that sneaky two-faced look while he did it.

We had another short letter from L, confirming his plans and giving us a date when he would arrive. So Tony and I went over to get the second place ready, with only a little less faith this time, because after all it seemed like a boon at this point to be having a visitor. The cherry trees were foaming all pink and white again in the glade, and lances of spring sunlight stood tall among the trunks, and the sound of birdsong was in our ears while we worked; and we talked about the year that had more or less exactly passed since we had first made these preparations for L and had expected him so innocently. Tony admitted that since then, he himself had started willing L to come, and I couldn't have been more surprised to hear it, nor more cognisant of the fatal weakness that is love, for Tony is not someone who interferes lightly in the course of things, knowing as he does that to take on the work of fate is to incur full responsibility for its consequences.

One of the difficulties, Jeffers, in telling what happened is that the telling comes after the fact. This might sound so obvious as to be imbecilic, but I often think there's just as much to be said about what you *thought* would happen as about what actually did. Yet – unlike the devil – these apprehensions don't always get the best lines: they're done away with, in about the time it takes to do away with them in life. If I try, I can recall what I expected of the meeting with L and what I thought it would be like to be near him and to be living alongside him for a period. I imagined it, somehow, as dark, perhaps because his paintings have so much darkness in them and his use of the colour black is so strangely vigorous and joyful. I believe also that I dwelt, in those few weeks, on the dreadful years before I met Tony, which I no longer thought about very often. Those years began, so to speak, with L's paintings and my fevered encounter with them that sunny morning in Paris. Was this then to be some stately conclusion to the evil of that time, a sign that my recovery was now complete?

These feelings led me to talk with Justine, in the days

before L's arrival, about what had happened more candidly than I ever had. Not that a parent's candour guarantees all that much! I believe that as a rule children don't care for their parents' truths and have long since made up their own minds, or have formulated false beliefs from which they can never be persuaded, since their whole conception of reality is founded on them. I can credit any amount of wilful denial and self-deception and calling a spade an apple tree among family members, because thereby hangs our self-belief by the slenderest of threads. There were certain things, in other words, that Justine could not afford to know, and so she would not let herself know them, even though her twin motivations – to be close to me at all times, and to remain suspicious of me – were always contradicting one another.

I have never needed particularly to be right, Jeffers, nor to win, and it has taken me the longest time to recognise what an odd one out this makes me, especially in the field of parenting, where egotism – whether of the narcissistic or the victimised kind – runs the whole show. It has sometimes felt as though, where that egotism should have been, I had only a great big vacuum of authority to offer. My attitude to Justine has been more or less the same as all my attitudes: dictated by the stubborn belief that the truth, in the end, will be recognised. The trouble is, that recognition can take a lifetime to arrive. When Justine was younger there had been a feeling of malleability, of active process, in our relations, but now that she was a young woman it was as though time had abruptly run out and we were frozen in the positions we had happened to assume in the moment of its stopping, like the game where everyone has to creep up behind the leader and then freeze the second he turns around. There she stood, the externalisation of my life force, immune to further alterations; and there was I, unable to explain to her how exactly she had turned out the way she had.

Her relationship with Kurt, however, offered a whole new angle on the subject. I've said that he adopted this attitude of prior knowledge when I was there, and I took this to represent the sum total of everything Justine had told him about me that he was unqualified to know. At first he also treated Tony as a special case, a kind of exotic alien, and had the infuriating habit of wearing a tiny crescent smile on his lips whenever he watched Tony going about his business. Tony responded by dealing the card of masculinity, and forcing Kurt to take it.

'Kurt, can you help me load up the woodpiles?' Tony would say, or 'Kurt, the fences in the bottom field need repairing and it's a two-man job.'

'Of course!' Kurt would say, with a somewhat ironic air, scrambling out of his chair and carefully rolling up the hems of his beautifully pressed trousers.

Predictably, he soon developed a childlike attachment to Tony in this mode, and started glorying in his own handiness and practicality, though Tony wasn't going to let him off that easily.

'Tony, shall we rake over the beds down by the orchard? I've noticed the weeds are starting to come through,' he would say, when Tony was sitting reading the paper or otherwise unoccupied.

'Not now,' Tony would reply, completely unperturbed.

You see, Jeffers, Tony refuses to see anything as a game, and by being that way he reveals how much other people play games and how their whole conception of life derives from the subjectivity of the game-playing state. If it sometimes means he can't altogether join in the fun, it doesn't matter: the needle always swings back in his direction, because in the end living is a serious condition, and without Tony's common sense and practicality the fun would run out fairly quickly in any case. But I like fun and want to have it, and I'm not practical the way Tony is, and so I have often found myself with nothing to do. Nothing to do! It has been my cry ever since I came to live at the marsh. I seem to spend a lot of time simply – waiting.

I decided to try to get to know Kurt, and found myself meeting an insurmountable obstacle straight away.

'Kurt, what is your home like?'

'I am lucky enough to come from an unbroken home.'

'What does your mother do? How does she spend her time?'

'My mother is at the top of her field, as well as having successfully raised a family. I admire her more than anyone else I know.'

'And your father?'

'My father has built his own business and is now free to do the things he enjoys.'

And so on, Jeffers, ad infinitum – all these positives, each one with a tiny shard inside that felt like it had been put there just for me. Justine was surprisingly propitiatory and little-womanish toward Kurt, and would drop whatever she was doing and rush around at the merest word from him. Sometimes, watching them walk together through the glade or down toward the marsh, their heads inclining, they looked to my eyes almost elderly, a little old man and woman taking stock on the far shore of life. She even took him tea in bed in the mornings! But they had both lost their jobs, and they needed money, and however much we liked to have them there, until they came up with a new plan they were living off our land and off our dollar – and we all knew it.

L wrote to say that he would be arriving by boat! We were somewhat mystified by this announcement, since most of the long-distance passenger boats still weren't running in that period and we had imagined he would come some other way. But there it was – he said he would be arriving at the harbour town about two hours' drive south of us, and were we able to pick him up?

'Must be a private boat,' Tony said with a shrug.

The day came and Tony and I got in the car, leaving Justine and Kurt to their own devices until evening, when we would be back. They agreed to have dinner ready for us, and I wondered what that dinner would be like with L there. The 'car' isn't really a car, Jeffers, more of a truck – a box-like old thing with enormous wheels that can go through or over anything and that is therefore very practical, except on the open road, where it starts to shake and judder as soon as you go more than forty miles an hour. Also the back seat is tiny, barely more than a bench, and I had already decided I would take it myself for the long drive home and allow L to sit in front with Tony. It was slow going, driving that distance, and Tony and I made sure to stop every now and then and get out, so that our shaken-up brains could settle down again. The road more or less sticks to the coast and the scenery is astounding from there, plunging and swooping all around, the great rounded green hills running right down to the sea with the ancient copses in their folds. It was the loveliest spring weather and when we got out of the truck the breezes coming up off the water were positively balmy. The sky was like a blue sail overhead and the waves crashed on the shore below and the water had that coruscation of the surface that is the surest omen of summer. How fortunate we felt to be there together, Tony and I – the debt of our isolation is paid back in an instant by times such as these. That vertiginous green landscape so full of movement and light is a great contrast to the low-lying subtlety of our marsh, though it is just to the south of us: it always lifts us and energises us to go there, yet we don't go as often as we could. I wonder why not, Jeffers? The pattern of change and repetition is so deeply bound to the particular harmony of life, and the exercise of freedom is subject to it, as to a discipline. One has to serve out one's changes moderately, like strong wine. I had very little awareness of such things in my existence before Tony: I had no idea at all why things turned out the way they did, why I felt gorged with sensation at one minute and starved of it the next, where my loneliness or joy came from, which choices were beneficial and which deleterious to my health and happiness, why I did things I didn't want to do and couldn't do what I wanted. Least of all did I understand what freedom was and how I could attain it. I thought it was a mere unbuttoning, a release, where in fact – as you know well – it is the dividend yielded by an unrelenting obedience to and mastery of the laws of creation. The rigorously trained fingers of the concert pianist are freer than the enslaved heart of the music lover can ever be. I suppose this explains why great artists can be such dreadful and disappointing people. Life rarely offers sufficient time or opportunity to be free in more than one way.

We arrived at the town in good time, and ate our sandwiches sitting on the seawall, and then at the appointed hour went down to the port to find L. We stood in the arrivals area and asked what boats were scheduled to arrive, but no one seemed to know about anything that sounded like it might have L on board. We settled down for a long wait: since we weren't quite sure *how* he was arriving, we didn't expect much in the way of punctuality.

I ought to try to describe to you, Jeffers, what we looked like, so that you can imagine this arrival from L's point of view. Tony, at least, is not a usual-looking person at all! He is very big and tall, and strong from all the physical work he does, and he has long white hair that would never be cut unless I occasionally took the scissors to it. He says his hair turned white when he was still in his twenties. It is quite fine and silky, almost womanish, and has a faintly blue tint to it. He is dark-skinned, the only dark-skinned person for miles around, having been adopted as a baby by a marsh family. He has no idea what his origins are and has never tried to find out. His parents didn't tell him he was adopted, and no one else ever referred to it, and since they lived a life of considerable isolation he says it wasn't until he was eleven or twelve that he worked out what it meant that he was a different colour to them! I have seen photographs of Native Americans, and more than anything he looks like one of them, though how that could be I don't know. He is more of an ugly than a good-looking man, with the permanence and dignity of ugliness, but he makes a handsome entity overall, if you see what I mean. He has a big face with heavy prominent features, except for his eyes, which are small and hard and look like they're focused on something very far away. His teeth are crooked, from lack of visits to the dentist in childhood. He remembers his childhood as perfectly happy. He grew up near the house we live in now, and he didn't really go to school, since his parents had certain beliefs about education and taught him at home themselves. They had another, biological child, a boy the same age as Tony, and these two boys grew up side by side, one white and one dark. I have never met Tony's brother and know next to nothing about him, except that he left the marsh when he turned eighteen and hasn't come back. I sense that a falling-out happened between them, but I don't know what. I think Tony must have been his parents' favourite, from the few details he's given me. I wonder what it feels like, to adopt a child and then prefer it to one's own. It seems, somehow, completely understandable. The parents died, both at the same time – they drowned, Jeffers, in one of the tidal surges that sometimes burst along our coast and can wrong-foot even people entirely familiar with the terrain. It was summer and they were out on their boat together, and the sea rose up and swept them away. Tony is always out on the water in his boat too, fishing or setting crab and lobster traps, but I believe that deep down he is afraid of it.

Tony has never – as far as I'm aware – purchased an item of clothing, since his adoptive father and grandfather happened to be big men also and left behind them such a sufficient store that Tony has rarely opened the wardrobe and found himself lacking anything. It does, however, make for some eccentricities of dress: on this particular occasion – the drive to collect L – he was wearing one of his grandfather's three-piece suits, complete with tartan waistcoat and watch chain. With his enormous size and his long white hair and his dark, rough-hewn face, he must have looked quite uncanny – I'm so used to him I can't always tell. I myself was presumably dressed as I always am, in either black or white, I can't remember which. I like to wear soft, draping, shapeless clothes which I can add or remove in layers, depending on the weather. I have never understood clothes terribly well, and have found the element of choice especially unmanageable, so it was a great day for me when I realised I could just wear everything all at once, and that by limiting the colours to black and white I need never think about the aesthetics again.

You know what I look like, Jeffers, and I looked then much as I did before and do now. I've always felt rather fatalistic, looks-wise, as though I were shuffling and reshuffling the same old set of cards, though in the difficult years

44

before I met Tony I did lose a proportion of the deck in weight, which has never come back to me. That day at the harbour, the cards were dealt in the pattern of my fiftieth year. I had some creases on my face, but not all that many: the oily skin that plagued me in my youth has defended me at this stage of life from wrinkles, a rare instance of fairness in the human lot. My long hair had some grey in it, a horrible, witch-like combination, I always think, but Tony's one wish as far as my appearance goes has been for me not to cut or dye my hair, and he's the one that has to look at it, after all. That day, the day of L's arrival, I do remember being unusually aware of the feeling that I had never once lived in the moment of my beauty, to the extent that I possess any. It had always felt like something I might find, or something I had temporarily lost, or something I was pursuing – it had felt, occasionally, immanent, but I had never had the sensation of holding it in my hand. I see that I am suggesting, by saying that, that I believe other women do have that sensation, and I don't know whether that is really true. I have never known another woman well enough to know, with the internal kind of knowledge a girl might have, for instance, of her mother. I imagine, somehow, the mother handing it to the girl, the pearl of her particular beauty.

To return to the business of L's arrival: there we were, sitting in our plastic chairs in the arrivals area, when a man and a woman walked in through the main doors. Since we were expecting L to come from the other direction we didn't take much notice of them, but then I did look, and realised the man must be L! He came over and said my name enquiringly, and I stood up all flustered to shake his hand, and at the same moment he stepped aside and brought the woman forward and said:

'This is my friend Brett.'

So I found myself shaking hands not with L but with a ravishing creature somewhere in her late twenties, whose air of poise and fashion was entirely unequal to her surroundings, and who offered her varnished fingertips as blithely as though we were meeting not at the ends of the earth but at a cocktail party on Fifth Avenue! She began to talk, gushingly, but I was so wrong-footed I couldn't really hear what she was saying, and I kept trying to look at L but he had sort of hidden himself behind her. Tony had by then got to his feet. Tony is never any help in that kind of situation – he just stands there and says nothing. But I can't bear any form of social awkwardness or tension: I become blank inside, so that I'm no longer aware of precisely what is being said or done. So I can't tell you, Jeffers, what exactly was said by us all in those moments, only that when I introduced Tony to the young woman – Brett – she seemed astonished, and gave him the most frankly assessing, up-and-down look I had ever seen in my life! Then she turned to me and gave me the same look, and I saw that she was imagining me and Tony together sexually, and trying to work it out and see what it was like. She had a curious mouth that hung open in a kind of letter-box shape – the mouth of a comic-book gunman, I often thought afterwards. I caught little, piercing glimpses of L in those frantic moments, hiding and dodging there behind her. He was quite wiry and small – smaller than me – and seemed dapper and goatish, in white trousers rolled up at the cuffs and leather deck shoes and a fresh blue shirt and a colourful scarf tied around his neck. He was very well groomed and cared for, which surprised me. Also he had a kind of light, capering demeanour, when I had imagined him swarthier and heavier, and his eyes were nuggets of sky blue from which the most arresting light came. They shone out at me like two suns whenever they happened to meet mine.

Somehow I got them all out of the arrivals area and up the hill to the truck, in the course of which they managed to communicate that they had come not by boat but by private plane, Brett's cousin being some billionaire or other who owned one, and who had dropped them off the day before and then buzzed off somewhere else. They had spent the night at a hotel in town, which accounted for their fresh, groomed appearance that had so caught me off guard, since people usually arrive in our part of the world draggled at least to some degree by the effort it takes to get here. It also explained their lack of luggage, which they had stored at the hotel and which we agreed we would collect on our way. I found it strange to think that they had been here a whole day and night without my being aware of it – I don't know why, Jeffers, but it seemed to give them some kind of power or vantage point over us. We arrived at the truck, which is usually such a dependable and friendly sight, and I looked at it, and looked at Tony standing in his three-piece suit next to it, and a great misgiving went through me, the way lightning can pierce all the way through a tree from top to bottom and hollow out its core. Oh, it wasn't at all how I'd planned it! I feared, suddenly, that my belief in the life I was living wouldn't hold, and that all I'd built up would collapse underneath me and I'd be unhappy again – I didn't know, in that moment, how I was going to manage. The first thing, obviously, was the presence of the woman Brett, which had come as a complete surprise to us and which was already creating a second difficulty, by increasing the elusiveness of L. I immediately saw that he would use her as a foil and a shield, and had probably brought her along for that purpose, to protect himself from the unknown circumstances he was travelling into, which was tantamount to protecting himself from me!

I should add, Jeffers, that I didn't generally need or expect any special attention from my visitors, not even from L, in whom I'd had such a long interest and with whose work I had a particular rapport. But in an arrangement such as ours there are certain necessary conditions, without which a range of abuses becomes possible, and the safeguarding of our privacy and our dignity of life was the first and foremost of them. I had the impression, from various things he had said in the course of our correspondence, that L was not above accepting favours from his friends and acquaintances, of whom a large number appeared to be wealthy. We were far from poor, but we lived simply and in a great degree of trust with those around us – we weren't, in other words, offering him a high-class holiday, or a luxurious place to use as his own. All our visitors so far had understood this immediately and naturally and there had been an unmarked line where all of us had instinctively met, between privacy and togetherness. But looking at L and even more so at Brett, I wondered whether we hadn't for the first time invited a cuckoo into our nest.

The first thing was to try to get us all into the truck, and then, once we'd called at the hotel, to get their luggage in as well. They had a large number of suitcases and bags, and Tony spent a long time planning how to fit them in, while the rest of us stood on the road, casting around for things to say. L had turned his back to me and put his hands in his pockets, and stood looking down at the crashing sea while the breeze made his shirt billow and flap and his short, fine greying hair lie flat against his head. I was left with Brett, who I had already understood was an insinuating kind of person who liked to get herself into your bodily space and make herself comfortable there, like a cat winding itself around your leg and then leaping into your lap. She was English: I remembered L alluding in one of his letters to his 'English friend' and wondered if this was she. She talked a great deal but didn't very often say anything you could reply to, and she was, as I have said, ravishingly beautiful, so the whole thing felt rather in the way of a performance, with you as the audience. She had very blonde, soft, waving hair and an exquisitely moulded little face with a tipped-up nose and startling large brown eyes, and then that strange and violent mouth. She was wearing a tailored dress of patterned silk tightly belted at the waist, and a pair of red, very high-heeled sandals – I had been surprised by how quickly she had moved in them while we were walking up the hill. She kept offering advice to Tony about the suitcases and getting in his way, until L unexpectedly turned around and said gruffly over his shoulder:

'Keep out of it, Brett.'

Well, Tony did take the longest time to manage it, and at a certain point when it looked like we could finally leave he suddenly shook his head and took everything out and started again; and meanwhile the breeze had picked up and it was becoming cold, and I thought about the long jolting journey in front of us and about my quiet, comfortable house and garden and about how this could have been just a pleasant ordinary day, and all in all managed to feel quite miserable about what I had brought about. Finally we got in, with L and Brett crushed together into the bench seat after all and Tony and I in front, where I relied on the noise of the engine to make further conversation impossible. All the way home I nursed my impression that there had been some kind of crash or clash, and my head spun with all the jarring sensations and disharmonies it had thrown up, and I had the blank, dead feeling I always get at such times. Tony's face in profile, looking impassively out at the road ahead, is usually a great comfort to me when I feel this way, but on this occasion it almost made things worse, because I wasn't sure L and Brett would ever get the hang of Tony, nor he of them, and the last thing I wanted to have to do on top of everything else was explain them to each other.

I don't remember all that much about the journey – I have blotted it out – but I do recall Brett leaning forward at one point and saying into my ear:

'I can colour your hair for you to hide the grey, you know. I know how to do it so that no one would ever guess.'

She was sitting directly behind me, and had obviously had ample opportunity to scrutinise my hair from the back.

'It's really quite dry,' she added, and she even ran her fingers through it to prove her point.

I have mentioned, Jeffers, my relationship to commentary and criticism and the feeling of invisibility I very often had, now that I lived a life in which I was rarely commented on. I suppose I might have developed an oversensitivity or allergy to commentary as a result – whatever the reason, I could barely stop myself from screaming and lashing out at the feeling of this woman's fingers in my hair! But of course I simply drove those feelings down inside of me and sat there like an animal in dumb torment until we finally reached the marsh and could get out.

Justine and Kurt had done everything exactly as I had hoped – the trouble was, what I had hoped for no longer applied. They had lit the candles and the fires and decorated the table with the first spring flowers from the marsh, and filled the house with warmth and the good smells of cooking. They were completely unruffled, with that acceptingness of the young, by the presence of an extra person, and they laid an extra place for her, and before we sat down to eat I took L and Brett across to the second place to settle them in, while Tony drove the truck around to unload their luggage. How I wished I could just leave it all to him, and go and get into my bed and pull the covers over my head and not have to say another word! But it is not

51

Tony's business to change places with me, nor I with him. We are separate people, and we each have our separate part to play, and no matter how much I yearned on occasion for that law to be broken, I have always known that the very basis of my life rested on it.

When we opened the door to the second place and went in and turned on the lights, it all suddenly looked rather poor and shabby to me, as though with their smart luggage and expensive clothes and their air of acquaintance with luxury, L and Brett had imported a new standard, a new way of seeing, in which the old things could no longer hold their shape. The wooden cupboards and shelves looked rough and higgledy-piggledy and the stove and table and armchairs stood bleakly in the electric light. Our reflections glared out from the windows, for it was more or less dark by then and the curtains weren't drawn. I drew them, averting my eyes from the images the glass held. L looked around and said nothing, and there was nothing to say, though I had already understood it was physically impossible for Brett to repress her urge to comment, so was not in the least surprised when she gave a tittering laugh and exclaimed:

'It's a cabin in the woods, straight out of a horror story!'

You will remember, Jeffers, that L's fame came strongly at the beginning of his career, when he was only in his twenties. After that, it must have felt as though he'd been given some heavy object he had to carry around for the rest of his life. Such things distort the flow of experience and misshape the personality. He told me that he left his family home when he was still a child, fourteen or fifteen years old, and went to the city, though how he survived in that period I don't know. His mother had several children from a previous marriage and those older children had apparently attacked him and threatened his life in some way, and so he ran away. His father had been his friend and protector, but the father died, of cancer, I think.

They lived in a desolate part of the world, a small town plunked down in miles and miles of empty plain. His parents owned a slaughterhouse and the family lived across from it. Some of his earliest memories were of looking out of his bedroom window at the chickens in the yard, pecking at pools of blood. The violence of his early work that so shocked people and drew their attention, and that was

understood to be a production of societal violence generally, was probably rooted in this much more primitive and
personal source. I wonder whether this explains L's failure
to ever hit quite the right note with the critics again, since
they expected him to go on shocking them, when in fact
he had been introspective all along. So his celebrity and
his success were a sort of uphill trudge after that, always
accompanied by a sense of reservation and half-spoken
disappointment; yet partly because of his virtuosic talent
he never lost his prestige or his artistic honour, even as
painting went in and out of fashion over the years. He
survived those changes in taste, and people have often
wondered why he did, but I believe it was because he had
never prostituted himself to them in the first place.

I'm telling you all this, Jeffers, because it was what L
told me: I don't know if these facts about his childhood – if
facts they are – are generally known. It's important to me
that I only tell you about what I can personally verify, despite the temptation to enlist other kinds of proof, or to
invent or enhance things in the hope of giving you a better picture of them, or worst of all making you identify
with my feelings and the way I saw it. There's an art to
that, and I have known enough artists to understand that
I'm not one of them! Nonetheless I believe there is also a
more common ability to read the surface of life, and the
forms that it takes, that either grows from or becomes an
ability to attend to and understand the works of the cre-
ators. One can feel, in other words, a strange proximity to
the process of creation when one sees the principles of

art – or of a particular artist – mirrored in the texture of living. This might go to explain some of the compulsion I felt toward L: when I looked at the marsh, for instance, which seemed to obey so many of his rules of light and perception that it often resembled a painted work by him, I was in a sense looking at works by L that he had not created, and was therefore – I suppose – creating them myself. I'm unsure of the moral status of these half-creations, which I can only hazard is akin to the moral status of influence, and therefore a powerful force for both good and evil in human affairs.

I woke up early the morning after L's arrival and saw the sun rising pink and golden through the glade, and so I got up and left Tony still asleep and went outside. I felt a great need to soothe myself and reconnect with my place in the world, after all the jars and jolts of the previous day – and of course, in that lovely morning light, none of it seemed quite as bad as I had felt it to be. I walked down through the shining wet grass to the point at which the trees give way to a wide view of the marsh and where the old boat stands with its prow lifted, yearning out toward the sea. There was a high tide and the water had stretched out to cover the land, in that silent and magical way of the tides here, that is somehow like a body turning and stretching and opening in sleep.

There, standing beside the boat and looking at the same thing I was looking at, was L, and I had no choice but to go to him and greet him, despite the fact that I was not at all ready for an encounter and was still wearing my nightclothes. But I had already understood that this was to be the keynote of my dealings with him, this balking of my will and of my vision of events, the wresting from me of control in the most intimate transactions, not by any deliberate act of sabotage on his part but by virtue of the simple fact that he himself could not be controlled. Inviting him into my life had been all my affair! And I saw suddenly, that morning, that this loss of control held new possibilities for me, however angry and ugly and out of sorts it had made me feel so far, as though it were itself a kind of freedom.

He heard my approach and he turned and spoke to me. I have not mentioned, Jeffers, how quietly L spoke: it was a murmur, like the sound of voices in a next-door room, something halfway between music and speech. You had to concentrate to hear him. Yet while he spoke, that arresting light from his eyes kept you riveted to the spot.

'It's lovely here,' he said. 'We're very grateful.'

He was all fresh and clean-shaven, in a well-ironed shirt with another colourful scarf knotted at the throat. His mention of gratitude filled me instantly with shame, as though I had offered him something by way of a bribe which he had politely declined. It made the fact of his presence here entirely my responsibility, as I have said. I was used to our visitors either finding or feigning their own independence very quickly, and making it clear there was something – egotistically speaking – in it for them. L, by contrast, was behaving like a well-brought-up child who had been taken somewhere against his will.

'You don't have to be here,' I said, or rather heard

myself say, since it was the kind of thing I never usually said.

He looked startled, and the light in his eyes went out for a second and then came back on again.

'I know that,' he said.

'I don't want gratitude,' I said. 'It makes me feel dowdy and ugly, like a consolation prize.'

There was a silence.

'All right,' he said, and a mischievous smile came over his face.

I stood there in my crumpled nightdress, with my hair unbrushed and my bare feet growing cold from the dew, and felt I would like to have burst into tears – such strange, violent impulses were coming over me, one after another. I wanted to lie down and hammer my fists on the grass – I wanted to experience a complete loss of control, while knowing that I had lost control, in my exchange with L, already.

'I thought you would be coming alone,' I said.

'Oh,' he said softly, 'that's right, you did,' as though there were nothing more to it than that he had forgotten to inform me. 'Brett's all right,' he added.

'But it changes everything,' I wailed.

It is hard to convey to you, Jeffers, the sense of intimate familiarity I felt with L from that very first conversation, an intimacy that was almost kinship, as though we were brother and sister – almost as though we shared the same root. The desire I had to cry, to let myself go in front of him, as though my whole life until that moment had merely been a process of controlling myself and holding things in, was part of this overpowering feeling of recognition. I felt acutely conscious of my own unattractiveness, as I would in all my dealings with L, and I believe this sensation has some significance, painful though it is to recall it. Because I was not in fact unattractive, and certainly no more so then than at any other time of my life: or rather, whatever my object-value as a woman, the powerful feelings of ugliness or repulsiveness that beset me were coming not from some outward scrutiny or reality but from inside my own self. It felt like this inner image had suddenly become visible to other eyes, specifically L's, but also Brett's – the thought of her invasiveness and her suggestive commentary, in that state, was unbearable! I realised that I had had this ugliness inside me for as long as I could remember, and that by offering it to L, I was perhaps labouring under the belief that he could take it from me, or give me some opportunity to escape it.

Looking back on it now, I see that what I was experiencing might simply have been the shock of being confronted by my own compartmentalised nature. All these compartments in which I had kept things, from which I would decide what to show to other people who kept themselves in compartments too! Until then, Tony had seemed to me like the least divided person I had known: he had at any rate whittled it down to two compartments, what he said and did, and what he didn't say and do. But L felt like the first entirely integrated being I had encountered, and the impulse I had was to catch him, as though he were a wild creature that needed to be ensnared, while at the same time realising that his very nature was not to be caught, and that I would merely have to abide by him in a dreadful freedom.

He began to talk, turning his eyes away from me and out toward the water and the marsh, and I had to strain and stand very still to hear what he said. The sun had risen higher and was driving back the shadows of the trees across the grass where we stood, and the water was likewise advancing, and so we were held between them, in one of those processes of almost imperceptible change that occur in the landscape here, whereby you feel you are participating in an act of becoming. The stillness mounts and mounts, and the air becomes more and more charged with intensity, and finally the sea begins to give back its light like a shield. I cannot reproduce L's words for you, Jeffers: I don't think it's possible for anyone to retain an accurate record of that deep kind of talk in any case, and I am determined not to falsify anything, even for the sake of a narrative. He talked about his weariness with society and his continual need to escape it, and the problem this posed in determining any kind of home for himself. As a younger man his mild homelessness hadn't troubled him, he said, and in later life he had watched the people of his acquaintance create homes that were like plaster casts of their own wealth, with humans inside. Those structures sometimes exploded and sometimes merely suffocated their occupants – but personally, he could never be anywhere without sooner or later wanting to go somewhere else. The one place that was real to him was his studio in

New York, the same one he had had all the way through. He had built a second studio at his country house but he couldn't work there: it was like being in a museum of himself. He had recently been forced to sell that house, he told me, along with his house in the city, which left him back where he had been at the beginning, with just the original studio. Likewise he had never been able to build anything permanent with other human beings. He knew plenty of gluttons for living who gained and lost and gained again and lost again in such quick succession that they probably never even noticed that none of it lasted; and he knew, too, enough examples of the rot that could be concealed within an outward-seeming lastingness. What interested him was his suspicion not that he might have missed out on something, but that he had failed entirely to see something else, something that had ultimately to do with reality and with a definition of reality as a place where he himself did not exist.

He had been forced to go back and think again about his childhood in light of this, he said, though he had long since realised that the particular details of his life were so much clutter, from which the essence merely needed to be extracted and the specifics thrown away. Yet there was something there, he felt certain, that he had overlooked – something to do with death, which had been a prominent feature of his early life. Right from the start, he had taken from death the impulse to live: even the deaths of the animals in the slaughterhouse, which might have horrified another child, gave him time and again a sensation that was like a note being struck, a confirmation of his own being. He supposed his lack of horror and emotion could be attributed to the deadening that results from repeated exposure to something, but in that case he had been dead almost from the beginning. No, in the striking of that note there was something else, a feeling of equality with all things that was also an ability to survive them. He himself could not be fatally touched, or so he had always believed: he could not be destroyed, even as he was witness to the destruction. He had taken his survival as freedom, and run away with it.

I told him that Tony had also had early experience of death, and had responded the opposite way, by staying exactly where he was forever after. I had sometimes chafed at this rootedness, which I took at first for caution or conservatism, but it had shown me its resilience enough times for me to treat it with respect. I had great trouble respecting anything, I said, and instinctively rebelled against what was presented to me as immovable or fixed. In the period of difficulty before I met Tony, I told him, I was sent to see a psychoanalyst who drew a map of my character on a piece of paper. He thought he could sum it up, on a crumpled piece of A4! It was his gimmick, and I could tell he was proud of it. The psychoanalyst's map showed a central pillar of what appeared to be objective reality, around which numerous arrows shot off into space and then met and crossed over to form an endlessly conflicting circle. Half these arrows were obeying the impulse to rebel, the other half the impulse to comply, the suggestion being that as soon as I was brought into compliance with something I rebelled against it, and having rebelled, felt a great urge to comply again – round and round in a pointless dance all of my own! He thought his explanation was sheer genius, but at that time I was possessed only by the desire to harm myself: it had me by the throat like a dog. And so I stopped seeing the psychoanalyst, because I could see he wasn't going to get that dog off me. It grieved me to prove him right about rebellion, though, or so I supposed he had the satisfaction of thinking.

Months later I met the psychoanalyst in the street, I told L, and he came over and with a little air of reproach asked me how I was, and I stood there in broad daylight and denounced him. I spoke as though some god of speech had taken possession of me on the pavement – I declaimed, the sentences falling from my mouth in great wreaths of significance. I reminded him that I, the mother of a young child, had come to him in distress, afraid that I might destroy myself, and he had done nothing, nothing to safeguard her or me, just doodled on a piece of paper and come up with the proof of my authority complex – as though I didn't have proof enough from the suffering I was in! Partway through my speech the psychoanalyst raised his arms in a gesture of surrender: he had turned completely white, and looked suddenly frail and aged, and began stepping backwards away from me on the pavement with his arms still raised, until he was far enough to turn and run. The image of this running man, I said to L, with his arms raised in surrender, had remained with me as the representation of everything I had failed to reconcile myself to. For me, there was no escaping my physical body. But he could simply run away!

L was listening, with his bright eyes fixed on mine and his hand over his mouth.

'How awfully cruel,' he said, though because of his hand I couldn't tell whether he was smiling or frowning, nor which of us he was accusing of cruelty.

We stood in silence for a while, and when L spoke again it was to resume the account of his childhood, so that it was as if my interruption were being politely set aside. I don't think this was because L was incapable of taking an interest in other people – he had listened carefully to my story, I felt sure. But the game of empathy, whereby we egg one another on to show our wounds, was one he would not play. He had decided to explain himself to me, that was all, and it was up to me what I offered in return. I understood I was not the first person to have received this explanation – I could imagine L being interviewed in a gallery or on a stage, giving much the same account of himself. A person only speaks like that when they feel they have earned the right to. And I hadn't, at least in his eyes – or not yet!

He began to tell me about a time in his childhood when his father had fallen ill, and he was sent away to live with an aunt and uncle for a time, to lessen the burden on his mother. This couple had no children of their own and were a rough and rambunctious pair of characters, he said, whose chief entertainment and motivation lay in each seeing the other meet with misfortune. He remembered watching his uncle howl with satisfaction and rub his hands together when his aunt burned herself on the oven; she would double over with laughter if he banged his head on the doorframe, and when they argued, chasing each other around the kitchen table with the poker or the frying pan, they could cheerfully draw blood. He wasn't sure the concept of character, as illustrated by these two, even existed any more. They were rather like animals, and it made him wonder whether character itself was an animal quality that humans had become distanced from in the modern age. His uncle and aunt didn't care especially about him, though they wouldn't have hurt him, and neither did they have any idea how to comfort him in this difficult period of his father's illness: he was expected to do his share of the hard physical work on top of his schoolwork, and indeed after a while they stopped sending him to school at all. He gradually came to realise that if his father died while he was staying at his uncle and aunt's house, they would very likely merely shrug at the news and carry on. They might even fail to tell him, and he was desperate to return home before this event took place, so clearly could he imagine it. He did succeed in getting home, and by the time his father died he had forgotten about his uncle and aunt, but it came back to him later, this time he had spent among people for whom he had no particular significance, and the urgent need he had felt to return to where he could play his role in the story. It was a clearer glimpse of death than any of the bloodier sightings he had had of it so far. He had discovered that reality would occur whether he was there to see it or not.

The sun had risen up above us by now and we stood together and looked out at the marsh and the loveliness of the day, and I felt the rare peace of living entirely – however briefly – in that moment.

'I hope we don't get in the way,' L said then. 'I'd hate to spoil this for you.'

'I don't see why you would spoil it,' I said, affronted again. How I wished he wouldn't say such things!

'It's felt like my luck has run out, that's all,' he said. 'Things have been awfully sordid these past months. But now I'm starting to wonder whether I even care. The wheel could turn again, but I have the feeling I'm going back in time, not forward. I feel lighter every day. It isn't so bad, dispossession.'

I said that was a sensation only a man – and a man with no dependents – could enjoy. I managed not to add, Jeffers, that in addition it relied on the generosity of burdened people such as myself! But I might as well have said it, because he heard me anyway.

'Don't mistake my life for anything other than a tragedy,' he said softly. 'In the end I'm nothing more than a beggar, and I never have been.'

I didn't see it that way at all, and I said so. Not to have been born in a woman's body was a piece of luck in the first place: he couldn't see his own freedom because he couldn't conceive of how elementally it might have been denied him. To beg was a freedom in itself – it implied at least an equality with the state of need. My own experiences of loss, I said, had merely served to show me the pitilessness of nature. The wounded don't survive in nature: a woman could never throw herself on fate and expect to come out of it intact. She has to connive at her own survival, and how can she be subject to revelation after that?

'I've always thought you didn't need revelation,' he murmured. 'I thought you somehow already knew.'

There was something sarcastic in his tone when he said that: in any case, I do recall him trying to make a joke out of this idea of women possessing some divine or eternal knowledge, which was tantamount to saying he didn't need to bother about them.

He said he was thinking of trying his hand at portrait-painting while he was here. Something about his change in circumstances was making him see humans more clearly.

'I wanted to ask,' he said, 'if you thought Tony would sit for me.'

This announcement came so much out of the blue and was so contrary to what I was expecting that I took it almost as a physical blow. There we stood in front of the very landscape I had looked at through his eyes and seen his hand in for all these years, and he turns around and says he wants to paint Tony!

'Also Justine,' he went on, 'if you think she'd play along.'

'If you're going to paint anyone,' I cried, 'then surely it ought to be me!'

He looked at me with a faintly quizzical expression.

'But I can't really see you,' he said.

'Why not?' I asked, and I believe it was the utterance that lay at the furthest bottom of my soul, the thing I had always been asking and still wanted to ask, because I had never yet received an answer. And I didn't receive an answer that morning either, Jeffers, because just then the figure of Brett could be seen approaching across the grass, and my conversation with L was thereby brought to an end. She was holding a bundle in her hands, which turned out to be all the linen from the bed in the second place, and she tried to offer it to me as I stood there in my nightdress on the wet grass.

'Would you believe it,' she said, 'but I can't sleep against this fabric. It irritates my skin – I woke up this morning with a face like a broken mirror! Do you have anything softer?'

She stepped closer, across the line that generally separates one person from another, when they're not intimately acquainted. Her skin looked perfectly fine even at close quarters, glowing with youth and health. She wrinkled her little nose and peered at my face.

'Do you have this fabric on your bed too? It looks like it might be having the same effect on you.'

L ignored this basic piece of effrontery, and stood with his arms folded looking at the view, while I explained that all our bedlinen was the same, and that its slight roughness was the result of it being an entirely natural and healthful product. I could not, I added, offer her anything else, unless I were to drive all the way back to the same town from which we had collected them the day before, where there were shops. She looked at me imploringly.

'Would that be completely impossible?' she said.

Well, somehow I got myself away – it was amazing how Brett could make you feel physically trapped, even in the most open of spaces – and ran back up to the house and threw myself into the shower and washed and washed, as if in the hope I'd be all gone by the time I was finished. Later I sent Justine and Kurt over to them, to get a list of any supplies they might need that could be bought in the small town closest to us, and if the subject of the bedlinen came up again, I never got to hear about it!

Justine was twenty-one years old that spring, Jeffers, the age at which a person begins to show their true colours, and in many ways she was revealing herself to be not at all who I had believed her to be, while at the same time reminding me unexpectedly of other people I had known. I don't think parents necessarily understand all that much about their children. What you see of them is what they can't help being or doing, rather than what they intend, and it leads to all kinds of misapprehensions. Many parents, for instance, become convinced that their child has artistic talent, when that child has no intention whatever of becoming an artist! It's all so many stabs in the dark, the business of trying to predict how a child will turn out – I suppose we do it to make bringing them up more interesting and to pass the time, the way a good story passes the time, when all that really matters is that afterwards they're able to go out into the world and stay there. I believe they know this themselves better than anyone. I was never very interested in the concept of filial duty, or in eliciting maternal tributes from Justine, and so we got to these essentials fairly quickly in our dealings with one another. I remember her asking me, when she was thirteen or so, what I believed the limits of my obligation to her were.

'I believe I am obliged to let you go,' I said, once I'd thought about it, 'but if that doesn't work out, I believe I am obliged to remain responsible for you forever.'

She sat silently for a while and then she nodded her head and said:

'Good.'

Because of events in our shared history I had come to see Justine as vulnerable and wounded, when in fact her key characteristic is her dauntlessness. As a small child she had shown this quality, and so perhaps it is truer to say, Jeffers, that we can consider our job as parents to have been accomplished without fatal error or wrongdoing when the small child becomes visible once more in the fully grown being. I have often considered the survival of paintings, and what it means for our civilisation that an image has survived across time undamaged, and something of the morality of that survival – the survival of the original – pertains, I believe, to the custody of human souls too. There was a period in which I lost Justine and during which I will never know precisely what happened to her, and it was for signs of damage from this time that I was always on the alert. I told her this, around the time that we had the conversation about obligation. I told her that she had lost a year of the care she was owed by me, and that she could consider it a formal debt, to be reclaimed at any time. I even wrote an IOU out for her on a piece of paper! She laughed at me for it, though not unkindly, and I was never handed back that piece of paper, but when she and Kurt returned from Berlin to live with us, it did occur to me that she was perhaps calling in what I owed her.

She had become somewhat of a stranger to me in her time away, and just as a familiar place can seem smaller and clearer when you return there after an absence, and any changes quite shocking at first, I found her somehow distilled, as well as in certain ways startlingly altered. Change is also loss, and in that sense a parent can lose a child every day, until you realise that you'd better stop predicting what they're going to become and concentrate on what is right in front of you. In that period her small, sturdy physique had suddenly matured, and acquired a density and agility that brought an acrobat to mind: she seemed full of a pent-up but expertly balanced energy, as though at any minute she might whirl exultantly up into the air. Yet likewise when she had no direction or nothing to do she could assume an awful flaccidity, like an acrobat who has somehow got herself stranded down on the ground. She had dismayed me by cutting off all her hair, and had taken to wearing squarish smocks and workaday clothes that stood in stark contrast to her physical ebullience, as well as to the splendour of Kurt's own wardrobe. I suspected that she was engaged in the pointless squandering of her femininity, and perhaps because I secretly feared I was somewhere to blame for it, I was tempted to lay this wastage at Kurt's door. The image of middle-aged dullness they formed seemed like something he, rather than she, had summoned up and was doing rather well out of, and I was frequently shocked by little put-downs and criticisms he would deliver to her in a quiet voice, the way parents sometimes lower their voices to criticise their children in front of other people, as a way of burnishing themselves. Yet Justine was slavish in her treatment of him, and would become quite frantic if his needs or expectations were frustrated by a particular turn of events, which meant that I was always slightly nervous while living at close quarters with them in the main house, lest I inadvertently be the cause of the frustration.

Privately, I interpreted Justine's conduct as the unmediated product of her feelings about her father, around whom I myself had once been nervous and slavish too, and in fact I had found myself beginning to substitute Kurt for him quite naturally. One morning I was sitting beside Justine while she was looking for something in her purse, and a small photograph fell out. I picked it up and saw a close-up image of her with her father, whom I had not seen in person for several years. Their heads were resting together and their arms were around one another's necks and they both looked very happy, and I was so astonished that I couldn't even feel envy or insecurity, just simple admiration!

'What a lovely picture of you with your dad,' I said to her, and jumped out of my skin when she screeched with laughter in my ear.

'That's Kurt!' she said, cackling and stuffing the photo back in her purse.

Later she told Kurt about it and they laughed again over the idea that I had mistaken him for her father, though I was gradually becoming aware that the misapprehension ran deeper in me than either of them realised. Whenever Tony asked Kurt to help outside, for instance, I would feel a protest leap immediately into my throat, as though I believed that Kurt should be shielded from discomfort and labour. I had believed the same thing of Justine's father, at one time, which shows how little we are able to truly change ourselves. Yet Justine herself didn't object to these requests, and the reason she didn't was because it was Tony who had made them, as I discovered when I myself once casually asked Kurt to help clear the dishes from the table and was treated to flounces and glares from Justine. I'm generally suspicious when people are said to 'adore' other people, especially when they've been given no choice over who those people are, but Justine did always seem to have taken to Tony right from the start and to have trusted him; and Tony, I believe, could not have loved Justine more had she been his own daughter. Most people are incapable of that disinterested kind of love, but Tony has no biological children and no blood relatives, and can love who he likes. He was determined, in any case, that Kurt should lend a hand and occupy himself. When I told him, mortified, about my mix-up over the photograph, he stopped what he was doing and stood as still as an alligator with his eyelids half-closed for the longest time, and I saw that the similarity between my choice of Justine's father and Justine's choice of Kurt had been evident to him all along.

That first morning after L and Brett's arrival, Jeffers,

when I stood and talked to L beside the boat, marked the beginning of a period of unseasonably hot weather. It was spring, which ordinarily is a time of turbulent change, when wind and sun and rain alternate to clear away the winter and germinate the new things. Instead we received day after day of inexplicable stillness and heat, and the first flowers rushed up out of the raw earth and the trees hastily put on their foliage. Walking on the marsh, I noted dry paths that usually would have been boggy with mud, and clouds of buzzing insects everywhere, and the air shrilled and pulsed with birdsong as never before, as though all these creatures had been summoned up from the earth to some great and mysterious appointment ahead of time.

It was so dry that Tony grew worried some of the young trees and plants might die for lack of spring rain, and so he started to build an irrigation system out of long lengths of rubber hose that he laid all around our land. It had so many circuits and junctions that it resembled a huge network of veins, and he had to pierce all the hoses with hundreds of tiny holes along their sides so that the water would come out in continuous drips. It was fiddly and laborious work and it took him many hours, and I got used to seeing him at a distance, now in one corner of the land and now in another, bent over in concentration. After a while he conscripted Kurt to help him, and then there were two tiny figures in the distance, bending and conferring, while the sun shone down on their heads. Every now and again I would bring them something to drink and it took them forever to notice I was there, while they puzzled out the mechanics of some complicated junction or tried to work out why water wasn't flowing down a particular tributary. They couldn't afford to be slapdash or careless: the smallest mistake would result in the failure of the whole system. Tony had planted most of those trees himself and he cared about each one. How arduous and time-consuming it is, Jeffers, to take care of every last thing and not deceive yourself and wave away some aspect of it! I suppose the writing of a poem must work along similar lines.

Kurt was willing enough to do the work at first, but after a while I could see that he was growing bored of it. He was relying on his good manners and on the mild discipline of his privileged upbringing to carry him along, rather than on the mania of the perfectionist or the tenacity of the dutiful soldier. His character – that of a cherished, well-trained house dog – struggled to accommodate this turn of events, in which it was hard to discern a narrative wherein he played the central role, and since he was exhausted by the end of the day in any case, he retreated into a kind of dazed blankness, as though he had received a sort of concussion to his sense of self-importance. The hiatus gave Justine a desire to experiment with her own power, for which Brett was ready and willing to provide the opportunity.

'Brett is such an interesting person,' Justine said to me one afternoon, when she had gone to get supplies for the second place and taken an unusually long time returning. 'Did you know that she danced in the London ballet, all the time that she was putting herself through medical school?'

I had no idea that Brett had been to medical school, nor that she was a trained dancer: all I knew was that at this current moment she was lodged like a giant splinter in my life, and that I had no idea how or when I was going to prise her out again.

Because of the unusually fine weather, in the evenings Tony would light the fire in the big brazier outside at dusk, so that we could sit and watch the sun set over the sea while the coolness of night came in. I would watch the smoke roll up into the sky, knowing that L could see it from the second place and hoping it would draw him to us. After that first conversation I had barely seen L, and any questions or requests from that household came through Brett, so that it couldn't have been made clearer to me that he was hiding. Each night Tony built the fire bigger and bigger, as if he had read my mind and was trying to help summon L himself. On the fourth or fifth night, just as darkness was about to fall, I finally saw the two of them winding their way through the shadows of the trees toward us. We all jumped up to welcome them and made room for them around the fire. I can't remember what we talked about, just that I was aware of L's lamp-like eyes, growing brighter and more penetrating as the dusk fell, like the eyes of some nocturnal animal – and also that he had made sure to sit as far away from me as he could possibly get.

We had a cocktail of some sort in a big jug which we were sharing around, but L didn't drink his: he accepted a portion, so as not to draw attention to himself, I suppose, and I found it afterwards, untouched. He never drank alcohol in the time that I knew him, at least that I saw. We always like to have a good drink at the day's end, Jeffers, and go to bed sleepy and not too late, along with the birds – it seems to suit our way of life here. So L's alertness in the darkness was unnerving. I was happy, though, to be in his presence, or more accurately, it was pleasant for an hour or two not to have to puzzle over what his absence meant. But then after that first time he didn't come again. He stayed at home, while Brett came tripping and calling through the glade to sit in a circle with us every night, usually next to Justine. Kurt, after his day spent with the hosepipes, would be nodding in sleep in front of the brazier before he was halfway through his first cocktail: we woke him up to eat his dinner but he mostly crept off to bed by nine. This left Justine at a loose end, and Brett was right there to pick it up. And so the fire by which I had hoped to summon what I wanted ended by summoning the very thing I didn't want, which was more of Brett's company!

After the incident with the bedlinen I had treated Brett with a cordial wariness whenever we chanced to meet, but now she began to spend more time in the main house and I saw that I would have to find a more serviceable manner for dealing with her. One afternoon I was passing Justine's room, and behind the closed door I heard the two of them talking and laughing inside. When I saw Justine later, her short hair was done in a new – and far more flattering – style, and she wore a bright scarf tied around her head that framed her pretty face quite strikingly.

'Brett's persuaded me to grow my hair,' she said, slightly shamefaced, for I had been dropping hints on that score for weeks.

And indeed she did grow out her hair, Jeffers, all through the spring and summer, and by the autumn her lovely dark curls were falling almost to her shoulders, though by then Kurt was no longer there to see them.

Soon she and Brett were always together, and since they weren't, I reasoned, all that far apart in age, I somewhat grudgingly supposed it was natural for them to become friends, despite being such different characters. In fact Brett was considerably older, as I discovered later, which might explain why Justine fell under her influence, rather than the other way around – to good effect, I must admit, at least as far as her appearance was concerned.

'What on earth is this?' Brett would say, as I myself didn't dare to, when she discovered Justine in one of those sack-like garments she had taken to wearing. 'Did it come from Mother Hubbard's cupboard?'

A 'Mother Hubbard' was that loose kind of dress certain Victorian ladies used to wear that covered them from top to toe, to avoid having to put on a corset – Brett's comparison was an exaggeration, but it wasn't far off! Brett herself, of course, showed off her lovely figure at every opportunity. I believed, I suppose, that Justine's concealment of herself and her embracing of the cult of plainness and comfort was the result of her shame and self-dislike, and the reason I believed it was because it was what I had always felt myself. At heart I feared I had failed to do something vital with respect to Justine's womanhood, or worse, had inadvertently done to her the same thing that had been done to me. I had grown up disgusted by my physical self, and regarding femininity as a device – like the corset – to keep the repellent facts from view: it was as impossible for me to accept what was ugly in myself as to accept any other kind of ugliness. A woman such as Brett, therefore, unnerved me deeply, not only because she relished self-exposure but because I sensed she was thereby capable – without especial malice – of exposing other people. So when one day in the kitchen she crept up behind Justine and, laughing, grabbed her smock by the hem and whipped it over her head, so that there in the kitchen my daughter's young body was revealed in its underwear for all the world to see, I was rather too ready to prove that Brett's game was up.

'How dare you?' I cried, which was what I had wanted to say to her since the day we had met. 'Who do you think you are?'

Justine was emitting muffled shrieks, which I soon understood were indicative of laughter, but all the same I was furious and upset, just as if it had been my own flesh that Brett had unveiled so mercilessly.

'I'm sorry,' Brett said, putting her pretty, remorseful face too close to mine and her conciliatory hand on my arm. 'Was that too high-spirited?'

'We're not all exhibitionists here,' I said, spitefully.

Justine, however, wasn't angry with Brett at all after that incident, and even allowed herself to be called Mother

Hubbard on occasion, which I privately fumed at until I realised one day that the sackcloths were no longer in evidence and that my daughter was undergoing a transformation. I came out of the house into the bright sunlight one afternoon and saw two figures sitting on the grass, and for a moment I didn't seem to know either of them – two fresh and laughing young women, their limbs bared to the sun, like a pair of nymphs in the dawn of the world who had alighted on our lawn!

'Brett wants to teach me to sail,' Justine said soon afterwards. 'Do you think Tony would let us use the boat?'

'You'd better ask him yourself,' I said. 'Are you sure she really knows what to do? It's not like motor-boating on the Mediterranean out there. I think he'd be worried.'

'She once sailed single-handed across the Atlantic!' Justine burst out when I made these objections. 'They even put on an exhibition in New York of the photos she took of the journey!'

Well, I could barely stop myself from unmasking Brett as a fantasist there and then, and forcing Justine to acknowledge the outlandish nature of her claims about her own life, but it seemed reasonable enough to expect that the facts would come to light on their own. I left it to Tony to shine that pitiless torch on Brett, and I felt secretly guilty that I had allowed Justine to become attached to someone who lied and aggrandised herself, as well as chagrined to remember that it was L who had brought her uninvited into our midst.

'She can do it,' Tony very much surprised me by saying,

after I had forced him to go and talk to Brett about sailing the boat. 'She's got the certificate. She showed it to me.'

This was an international qualification, Jeffers, that apparently enabled the holder to skipper large-sized yachts anywhere in the world. Our old wooden dinghy barely counted! Justine had always loved going out on that boat with Tony, though she had resisted his own attempts to teach her how to sail it. I think it would be true to say that she wasn't sure the adults in her life could teach her anything, not even Tony. But also she couldn't see the point of learning, she had said, since she would be unlikely ever to keep a boat of her own, and Kurt had seemed to reinforce that outlook, in which fear masqueraded as common sense or even disdain. I could almost see him thinking that if Justine learned to sail, she might one day just get in a boat and sail away from him! In this and other ways she and Kurt had seemed to be turning their backs on risk and adventure. But now I saw her begin to rebel against these prescriptions, even as I had privately resigned myself to them and to the future in which they had promised to confine her.

What I am trying to say, Jeffers, was that in watching Justine begin to separate herself from Kurt and question his control over her, I was in the strangest sense watching her overtake me, as though we were running a race, at different points in time but over the same terrain, and in the place where I had catastrophically fallen she leaped with superior skill and strength and ran on. The resemblance I saw between Kurt and her father was a striking product

81

of my unconscious mind, because I was frightened of the latter and therefore saw him as something menacing and large, whereas Kurt I dismissed as clinging and weak. But Kurt wasn't weak: men never are. Some of them admit their strength and use it to the good, and some of them are able to make their will to power seem attractive, and some of them resort to deception and connivance to manage a selfishness of which they are themselves somewhat frightened. If Kurt was weak, in other words, then so had Justine's father been, and this was what the incident with the photograph had revealed to me. So much of power lies in the ability to see how willing other people are to give it to you. What I had dismissed as weakness in Kurt was the same force that had ravaged my life all those years before, and which even now I had only recognised by mistake.

Those first weeks of L's visit, while Tony laid the irrigation system and Brett trespassed into our lives and the hot weather held us in a kind of thrall, had a quality of intermission or interval, and the changes that occurred were like the changes of costume and scenery that go on backstage. And there was I, an audience of one in the stalls: it felt, almost, as though I were looking at it all through the wrong end of a telescope and seeing things from a greater distance than I usually did, perhaps because I myself was not especially the focus of anyone's attention. These periods can feel like intimations of death, until one remembers that it is the presence of the audience that allows the whole show to be put on in the first place. But I was aware of an empty seat next to mine, where L should have been: I felt we could have watched and understood together. My disappointment and my sorrow were held in check by the hope that soon he might reveal himself.

Because Tony was so busy with the hosepipes he didn't have time to plant out the spring seedlings in the vegetable garden, and so I had to offer to do it myself, even though I dislike having to do work of this kind. This isn't out of laziness, but rather the feeling that my life has entailed too many practical tasks, so that if I add even one more to the total, the balance will be tipped and I will have to admit I have failed to live as I have always wished to. The trouble lay in finding anything to put on the other side of the scales: I was quite capable, as I have said, of spending all my free time just sitting and staring in front of me. And yet the second anyone asked me to go and do something, I immediately felt oppressed! Tony understood this about me entirely, and hardly ever expected me to move a muscle, and the only thing that irked him was that I couldn't expend more of this need for inactivity in sleep and in mental passivity. I always sprang out of bed in the morning, careening around full of energy and will and quite capable of building Rome in a day, only this other part of me wouldn't let me do it. Tony slept deeply and long, and when he rose he carried the balance of his pleasures and his duties along with him, so that he never strained any one part of himself with too much of either. I would watch him in fascination, Jeffers, trying to learn. He made and ate his breakfast with excruciating slowness, while I wolfed mine down like an animal, so that it was gone long before I had stopped feeling hungry. He would go to an immense amount of trouble over certain things that filled me only with impatience, like the broken old radio I had wanted to throw away but he was determined to fix, even though we had replaced it with a new one. He spent the longest time over it, and for a while our kitchen table was covered with all the parts, and then just as we had started to argue over it, it disappeared. A few days later I had to go and tell him something while he was down at the field on his tractor, and as I approached across the grass I distinctly heard an aria from Handel's *Alcina* pealing out over the noise of the engine. He had installed the machine in his tractor, so that he could listen to music while he drove up and down!

Tony believed that I had done more than my fair share of work, and that what was required of me now in my life with him was to enjoy myself, but what he hadn't reckoned with was the difficulty of finding pleasure and enjoyment for someone who has never really valued them. He thought I should take pride in what I had survived and what I had achieved, and go around like a sort of queen bee, but meanwhile I had come to view the world as far too dangerous a place in which to stop and congratulate myself. The truth was I had always assumed that pleasure was being held in store for me, like something I was amassing in a bank account, but by the time I came to ask for it I discovered the store was empty. It appeared that it was a perishable entity, and that I should have taken it a little earlier.

What I wanted now was work or distraction of a meaningful kind, but try as I might, I couldn't find meaning in those seedlings! Nonetheless I put on my old boots and found the trowel and rake, and with much sighing I trudged down to the vegetable beds to begin my task. Just as I was unloading the trays of little green shoots from the wheelbarrow, who should appear by my side but Brett, all fresh and lovely in a primrose-yellow dress, with silver sandals on her feet that offered the greatest possible contrast to the muddy, ogreish affairs on mine.

'Need a hand?' she said cheerfully. 'L's in a foul mood this morning, so I thought I'd better make myself scarce.'

Well, Jeffers, with all my irritation over Brett's presence and my feeling of being imposed upon, I admit I hadn't thought once about how it might be for her to be stuck out here among strangers, sharing a confined space with a man of famed intractability to whom her relationship was unclear. I'm not the kind of woman who intuitively understands or sympathises with other women, probably because I don't understand or sympathise all that much with myself. Brett had seemed to me to have everything, and yet in that moment I saw in a flash that she had nothing at all, and that her intrusive and uninhibited manner was simply her means of survival. She was like one of those climbing plants that has to grow over things and be held up by them, rather than possessing an integral support of her own.

'That's good of you,' I said, 'but I wouldn't want your nice clothes to get dirty.'

'Oh, don't worry about that,' she said. 'It's a relief to get dirty sometimes.'

She picked up the trowel and squatted down beside the trays of seedlings.

'If we dig a little trench,' she said, 'it will make it easier.'

I was quite happy to let her take charge, and I sat back on my heels while she made a low trench very deftly and neatly all along the bed. I asked her whether L was often bad-tempered, and she stopped what she was doing to throw her head back melodramatically and laugh.

'Do you know what he says? He says he's going through the change!'

'The change? Like a woman?'

'That's what he says. Except I don't think women actually use that word any more.'

I found this idea quite interesting, Jeffers, despite Brett's laughing at it: it seemed to me like something that might well happen to a creative artist, where a loss or alteration in the sources of potency had occurred. Oh, the bitter feeling of release from one's service to blood and fate! To be led and then discarded by one's urges: why should an artist not feel it more than anyone?

'If you ask me,' Brett said, 'it's everything else that's changing, not him. He preferred it like it was before. He's sulking, that's all. He wants back all the things he pretended to take for granted.'

The art market had completely collapsed, she went on, after years of crazed overvaluing, so there were a lot of people in the same boat as L – and far worse, because they didn't have his pedigree. But there were others – a small number – whose reputations and fortunes were surviving unharmed.

'Some of them happen to be younger than him,' she said, 'and a different colour, and a couple of them are actually women, which adds to his feeling that the world is against him. The trouble is, he feels impotent.'

'But he *is* somebody,' I said.

Brett lightly shrugged her shoulders.

'I think he was settling in for a long and luxurious retirement as an artistic eminence. He has a lot of rich friends,' she added, in a low voice. 'It would have taken him a whole year just to visit them all, and by the time he'd finished he'd be ready to go back and see the first one again. Most of them were heavy investors in his work, and if he paid them a call now, they'd all be sitting staring at walls that have had ninety per cent of their value wiped off them. I believe,' she went on, nimbly lifting the seedlings from their trays and starting to stand them in a line down the trench, 'this might be the best possible thing for him. To be stripped down to nothing again. He's too young just to sit drinking martinis by someone else's swimming pool.'

I asked her how old she was herself.

'I'm thirty-two,' she said, grinning, 'but you have to swear not to tell anyone.'

She told me that she had met L through her rich cousin, the same one who had flown them here.

'He's an awful creep,' she said. 'He used to shut me in a cupboard at family parties when I was little and put his hands up my dresses. He looks like a sea monster now. But he became a collector, as they all do. They have so little imagination, they don't know what else to do with their money. It's funny, isn't it, how determined they are to prove that the thing that can't be bought can in fact be bought after all. I actually first met L at his house, and then later I persuaded him to buy a whole tranche of sketches L had sitting around in his studio, and since he knows nothing about art he was happy to pay far too much for them and then fly us here into the bargain. That's all the money L has,' she added, 'for now.'

'And what about you?' I said, rather aghast at all this.

'Oh, I've always had money. A lot of it's gone, of course, but I have enough. That's been my problem. No motivation.' She grimaced and made quote marks with her fingers as she spoke the words. 'I was drawn to L because he seemed so bitter and angry and rebellious, and I hardly ever meet people like that in the world I live in. I didn't ask myself what he was doing there in that world himself!'

She told me how much she liked Justine.

'She has so much honesty,' she said. 'Did you make her like that?'

I said I didn't know. I'd certainly always been honest *with* her, but that wasn't quite the same thing.

'People can get tired of too much honesty,' I said. 'It makes them want to cover things up again.'

'It certainly does!' Brett said. 'By the time I was eleven, I was so tired of people showing me things they pretended weren't for my eyes, I decided to become a nun! I was always deciding to be things – I think I did it in the hope of finding something I couldn't do.'

She asked me how I'd met Tony and come to live out here, and I told her the story and about how it had happened entirely by chance. It was a strange thing, I said, to live a life that had no connection whatever to anything you'd ever done or been. There was no thread that led to Tony, and no path between here and where I was before, and so my knowledge of it and of him had to come from an entirely different source. There was a place not too far away, I told her, a sort of archipelago where the sea has made these great fissures into the land, and on opposite banks of one of these very long and narrow bodies of water there are two villages that face one another. It would take literally hours to get by road from one to the other, going miles and miles inland and then coming back out again, yet they can see one another so clearly, right down to the clothes hanging on each other's washing lines! Something of that separation, I said, which was composed not of distance but of impassibility, illustrated my own situation: I was more familiar with what I looked at than with where I actually was, and so I knew exactly what it would have been like to be over there, looking across at here. What I wasn't so sure of was what here looked like. But I knew I was lucky to have met Tony.

'It's frightening to live on luck,' Brett said, somewhat wistfully.

Then she asked me, straight out, if I thought I was in love with L!

'No,' I said, though the truth was, Jeffers, that I had been starting to wonder the same thing myself. 'I just want to know him.'

'Oh,' she said. 'I wondered what it was.'

'Are you in love with him?' I asked.

'I'm just a pal,' she said, dusting the earth off her hands and putting the empty trays back in the wheelbarrow. 'He was really crazy about me for a while. I think he thought I could fix him sexually, but I can't. He's all finished in that department. Instead I'm getting him to teach me to paint. He says I've got some ability. I think that's going to be my next career!'

Tony surprised me very much by saying that he was going to sit for L. He went across to the second place on a bright fresh morning, and returned several hours later.

'I don't know why that man doesn't just kill himself,' he said.

He gave L two more sittings, and after that he had too much work to do. Large shoals of mackerel had suddenly arrived in our waters, and he and the men were taking their boats out every day and then selling the catch. It meant we had fresh mackerel for dinner, and also that Tony was gone from dawn till dusk.

A parcel arrived for L, a large tattered box covered with foreign stamps, and since Brett and Justine had driven off to town together, I took it across to him myself. I hadn't set foot over there in all this time, and hadn't seen L alone since that first morning when we had stood by the prow of the boat and talked. It's hard to say exactly what I felt, Jeffers, except that there was a numb kind of disappointment inside me for which I could find no justifiable cause. Perhaps it was simply that although L and Brett had been with us for three weeks or so by then, we had absorbed their arrival without feeling any increase from it. Brett sailed gaily on the surface, while L had sunk like a stone into deep waters. I couldn't really have said what was wrong, or expounded on my disappointment and the expectations it had come from – we were used to such visits taking all kinds of unpredicted forms – and all I could think was that it somehow came back to the question of gratitude that had arisen right at the start, in that first conversation with L. I had never, I supposed, come across such a flagrant case of ingratitude as his, and what I remembered was that he had offered gratitude in the very first words he spoke to me and that I had spurned his offer.

The box was really quite an awkward and heavy thing to haul up the rise through the glade. The door to the second place stood open in the sun, and at the threshold I stopped and put the box down just inside and paused to get my breath back. From there I had a view of the windows that ran across the front of the big room, and I couldn't stop myself from crying out:

'My curtains!'

The curtains had vanished – just the bare poles remained! At the sound of my voice L, whom I hadn't even noticed sitting with his back to me in the far corner of the room, turned around. He was hunched on a wooden stool, wearing a great paint-stained apron, with a canvas on an easel in front of him. He had no brush or other implement in his hand: as far as I could tell, he had simply been sitting staring at it.

'We took them down,' he said. 'They got in the way.

They're quite safe,' he added, and then said something under his breath which sounded like *my curtains*, uttered in an unpleasant mocking tone.

The canvas in front of him was a muddy, indistinct ground with ghostly escarpment shapes cascading down into its centre. It was very faint, as if it was only just beginning to emerge, so it was difficult to decipher much about it except that its mountainous shapes bore no relation to what could be seen through the bare windows.

'That came for you,' I said, pointing at the box.

His expression lifted at the sight of it, and the light in his eyes came on.

'Thank you,' he said. 'It must have been heavy to carry.'

'I'm not a weakling,' I said.

'But you're very slight,' he said. 'You could have hurt your back.'

It may just have been the quiet and indistinct way he spoke, or it may have been my difficulty in accepting commentary on my person, but the instant he made that remark about my size I became unsure that he had said it at all – and remain unsure to this day! It was so characteristic of him, Jeffers, this blurring of the interface of what I can only call the here and now. Things became formless and impalpable, almost abstract, where normally they would sharpen into focus. Being with him in a particular time and place was the very opposite of being with other people: it was as if everything had either already happened or was going to happen afterwards.

'Someone had to bring it,' I said.

'I'm sorry,' he said. 'That's inconvenient for you.'

93

We stood and stared at one another, and if there's one thing I've learned from Tony it is a certain stamina for a contest of that kind. But in the end I was ready to admit defeat, and I started to say that I was going back to the house, when at exactly the same moment he said:

'Won't you sit down?'

He offered a stool next to his, but I went and sat in the old ladder-back chair beside the empty fire instead, a piece of furniture I have held on to throughout my adult life and that for reasons I have forgotten I had chosen to put there, in the second place. Perhaps it had reminded me too much of the life before Tony, and therefore didn't seem to belong in our home: whatever the reason, I was comforted to encounter it again that day, and to remember that it had existed before all of the things that were happening now, and would continue to exist in the future.

'We call that the electric chair,' L said. 'The shape is uncannily similar.'

'I'll have it taken away if you like,' I said coldly.

'Don't be silly,' he said. 'I was only teasing.'

Unmoved, I sat there and took my first good look at L. How can I describe him to you, Jeffers? It's so hard to say how people appear, once you've come to know them – far easier to say what it's like to be near them! When the east wind blows on the marsh it makes everything feel very cool and contrary, even in the warmest weather – well, L was something of an east wind, and like that wind he fixed himself to the spot and settled in to blow. Another thing about him was the way the question of male and female felt somehow theoretical in his

94

presence, I suppose because he made his disregard for convention so apparent. He undermined, in other words, one's automatic ideas about what men and women are.

He was very small and neatly made and not at all physically imposing, yet there was always the sense that he could burst out at any minute in some violent physical act – a feeling of impulses under continual restraint. He had a careful way of moving, as though he had been injured in the past, but in fact I think this was just the way age had come to him, perhaps because he had thought he would be young forever. And he did still seem youthful, partly because his features were so finely drawn, especially the dark brows arching markedly over the very wide-open eyes that were filled with the light I have described. His nose was small and aristocratic-looking: the nose of a snob. He had quite a sweet, small mouth with full lips. There was something Mediterranean in his appearance – a quality, as I have said, of sharp drawing. He was always very clean and groomed, not at all how one imagines an artist to be. By contrast his painting apron was the grisliest garment, caked with gore like a butcher's smock. I noticed for the first time that the fingers on his left hand were slightly deformed – they were crooked, and flattened at the tips.

'An accident in childhood,' he said, seeing me look at them.

Yes, he was an attractive man, though somehow illegible to me: he emanated a kind of physical neutrality that I took personally and interpreted as a sign that he did not consider me to be truly a woman. As I have said before, he made me feel acutely unattractive, and I admit I had dressed that day with care, anticipating that I might see him. Yet he was so diminutive and self-contained, not at all the sort of man I myself might be physically drawn to – I could have defended my vanity if I'd wanted to! Instead I succumbed to a feeling of abjection, within which there was an illogical sense of hope. I wanted him to be more than he was, or to be myself somehow less than I was, and because I wanted those things my will was aroused – in any case, there was the feeling of some unknown lying between us that awoke a dangerous part of me, the part that felt that I hadn't truly lived. It was this same part – or an aspect of it – that had drawn me to Tony, who likewise I hadn't entirely recognised at first or imagined myself attracted to. Tony also awoke me, but to the presence in myself of a fixed male image, to which he did not correspond. To see him, I had to use a faculty that I did not entirely trust. All my life this image, I came to realise, had in various forms caused me to recognise certain people and to consider them real, while others remained unnoticed or two-dimensional. I understood that I should no longer trust it, and the mechanism of not trusting and not believing and then being rewarded for it came over time to supplant my actual trust and belief: this, I think, more than Tony himself and more than the geographical distance from my previous life, formed a great part of the gulf separating me from the person I had been.

I have often wondered, Jeffers, whether true artists are people who have succeeded in discarding or marginalising their inner reality quite early on, which might explain how someone can know so much about life with one side of themselves, while understanding nothing about it at all with another. After I met Tony, and learned to override my own concept of reality, I became aware of how widely and indiscriminately I was capable of imagining things, and how coldly I could consider the products of my own mind. The only experience I had had of such a phenomenon in my previous life was the luridness with which, at a certain point, I had imagined doing some violence to myself: it was, I suppose, at this very point that my belief in the life I was living and my inability to live it any longer were fighting a sort of duel to the death. I believe I glimpsed something in those moments, a horror of or hatred for myself, that was like the threshold to a whole underside of personality: it was a monster I saw, Jeffers, an ugly, thrashing colossus, and I banged the door on it as fast as I could, though not fast enough to stop it taking a big gouge out of me. Later, when I came to live at the marsh and looked back on my memories, I found that I viewed myself in the cruellest light. Never have I yearned more to be capable of creating something than at that time. It felt as though only that – to express or reflect some aspect of existence – would atone for the awful knowledge I seemed to have acquired. I had lost the blind belief in events and the immersion in my own being that I realised had made existence bearable up to that point. This loss seemed to me to constitute nothing less than the gain of perceptual authority. It felt as though it was an authority beyond language: I was so certain I could visualise it that I even bought painting materials and set myself up in a corner of the house, but what I experienced there was the opposite of release, Jeffers. Instead it was as if a total and permanent disability had suddenly taken hold of my body, a paralysis within which I would have to live wide awake for evermore.

As Sophocles said it – how dreadful knowledge of the truth is, when the truth can't help you!

But my aim here is to give you a picture of L: my thoughts about perception and reality are useful only insofar as they advanced my clumsy understanding of who and what L was, and of how his mind worked. My suspicion was that the artist's soul – or the part of his soul in which he *is* an artist – has to be entirely amoral and free of personal bias. And given that life as it goes on works to reinforce our personal bias more and more in order to allow us to accept the limitations of our fate, the artist must stay especially alert so as to avoid those temptations and hear the call of truth when it comes. That call, I believe, is the easiest thing in the world to miss – or rather, to ignore. And the temptation to ignore it comes not just once but a thousand times, all the way until the end. Most people prefer to take care of themselves before they take care of the truth, and then wonder where their talent has disappeared off to. This doesn't have all that much to do with happiness, Jeffers, though it must be said that the artists I have known who have come closest to fulfilling their vision have also been the most miserable. And L was one such: his unhappiness stood around him like a thick fog. Yet I couldn't help but suspect that it was bound up with other things, with his age and fading manhood and the change in his circumstances: he wished, in other words, that he had taken *more* care of himself, not less!

He began to talk, sitting there on the stool, about a time he had spent in his younger years in California, just after the first dramatic peak of his early success. He had bought a place on the beach, so close to the water that the breaking waves would surge white and foaming almost into the house itself. The mesmerising sound and action of the ocean cast a kind of spell or enchantment, in which he had lived the same day over and over until he was no longer aware of their passing. The sun beat down and was frothed back up into a sort of mist by the pounding waves, to make an encircling wall of phosphorescence that was like a bowl of light. To live in a bowl of light, outside the mechanism of time – this, he recognised, was freedom. He was with a woman called Candy, and the edible-sounding sweetness of that name defined her – everything about her was pure delicious sugar. For a whole long summer the two of them lived on the sand and rolled in the luminous water, barely dressing, turning so brown it was as if something inside them had become eternal, like two clay figures baked in a kiln. He could spend all day just watching her, the way she stood or lay or moved, and he didn't draw her even once, because she seemed to have plucked that thorn from his heart and brought him to a condition of stunned intimacy. She was already the most accurate possible representation of herself, and he submitted to her like a baby submits to its mother, and the sweetness he got in return was a kind of narcotic that made him know for the first time what it was to be oblivious.

'She moved to Paris,' he said, pinioning me to my chair with his eyes, 'and she married some nobleman there, and I hadn't seen her or heard from her in decades. But last week she suddenly wrote to me. She got my details from my gallerist and she wrote to tell me about her life. She and her husband live in some out-of-the-way place in the country, and their daughter lives in the family house in Paris. The daughter is the same age Candy was that time when we lived on the beach, and it had made her think about those months again, because her daughter reminds her so much of herself at the same age. She had thought about trying to see me, she said, but in the end she decided not to. Too much time has passed, and it would be too sad. But if I found myself in Paris, she said, she was certain her daughter would love to meet me and show me around. I've been wondering,' L said, 'about how to get there, and about what it would be like to meet this girl. The mother reborn in the daughter – it's so wonderfully tempting, so preposterous! Could it possibly be true?'

He was smiling, a great chillingly luminous smile, and his eyes were blazing – he looked suddenly uncanny and alive, dangerously so. I had found his story painful and horrible, and I half hoped he had told it with the intention of being cruel, because otherwise I would have to conclude he was a madman! To rush off to Paris, an ageing man down on his luck, with the expectation of meeting a re-creation of his former lover and being gloriously restored to potency and youth – it would have been laughable, Jeffers, had it not also been so disturbing.

'I don't know about getting to Paris,' I said, rather stiffly. 'I don't know if it's possible. You'd have to find out.'

How I hated having that stiffness forced on me! Did he understand that by parading his freedom and the fulfilment of his desires in front of me, he was making me less free and less fulfilled than I had been before I walked in the door? He looked startled when I spoke, as though he hadn't expected me to raise such a practical objection.

'It's all so silly,' he said softly, half to himself. 'You get tired of reality, and then you discover it's already gotten tired of you. We should try to stay real,' he said, smiling that awful smile again. 'Like Tony.'

He gave a strange giggle, and pulled out the picture of Tony from behind the easel and leaned it up against the wall for me to see. It was a small canvas, but the figure was even smaller – he had made Tony tiny! He was shown full-length and in meticulous detail, like an old-fashioned miniature, all the way down to his shoes, so that he seemed both tragic and insignificant. It was merciless, Jeffers – he made him look like a toy soldier!

'I imagine you yourself see him like Goya would,' he said, 'at arm's reach. Or is it arm's length?'

'I've never seen Tony all at once,' I said. 'He's too big.'

'He didn't give me enough time,' he said brusquely, seeing my disappointment at the picture, just as I had intended he should. 'He seemed to be very busy.'

There was a certain mockery in that remark, as though he were accusing Tony of aggrandising himself.

'He only came because he thought I wanted him to,' I said miserably.

'I'm trying to find something in the figure, but perhaps it isn't there,' L said. 'Some brokenness or incompleteness.' He paused. 'You know, I've never wanted to be *whole* or *complete*.'

He was studying the picture of Tony while he spoke, as though it represented this wholeness that he couldn't or wouldn't attain and was therefore, perversely, a failure. It was a completing that betrayed the ongoing fragmentation or mutation of his own personality.

'Why not?' I said.

'I always imagined it was like being swallowed,' he said.

'Perhaps it's you that does the swallowing,' I replied.

'I haven't swallowed anything,' he said calmly. 'Just taken a few bites here and there. No, I don't want to be completed. I prefer to try outrunning whatever's after me. I prefer to stay out, like kids on a summer evening stay out, and won't come in when they're called. I don't want to go in. But it means that all my memories are outside me.'

He began then to talk about his mother, who he said had died when he was somewhere in his forties. He had always found her physically loathsome, he said – she was forty herself when she had him, her fifth and last child. She was very fat and coarse, where his father was delicate and small. He remembered the feeling that his parents didn't match, didn't go together somehow. When his father was dying, L was often alone at his bedside, and he frequently noticed fresh bruises and other marks on his father's skin that only his mother could have put there, since no one else visited the sickroom. He sometimes wondered whether his father had died just to get away from her, but he couldn't believe that his father would have wanted to leave him there by himself. He realised later how much his father had tried to keep him out of his mother's path, which is how L came to start drawing: while his father did the accounts or the yard work L was nearly always by his side, and it was something his father thought of to occupy him with.

His mother used to ask him to touch her: she complained that he never showed her any affection. He sensed she wanted him to serve her. He felt compassion for her, or at least pity, but when she asked him to rub her feet or knead her shoulders he was revolted by the physical reality of her. In this way she revealed to him what she wanted that no one would give her. He didn't count – for her, he had no real existence. He had a memory of standing as a small child at the kitchen window, making paper-chain figures out of old newspaper with a big pair of scissors, his father elsewhere, his mother doing something at the stove. The discarded scraps of paper rained down on the floor like snow as he cut. He remembered the sound of her voice, calling him over to hug her. Occasionally she would summon him in this way, as though her own loneliness had suddenly become unbearable to her. She had been strangely moved by the sight of the figures when he unfurled them, all joined together by the hands. She kept asking him how he had done it; he realised then that he had made her credit him with a certain power, because she didn't understand him.

'I remember always being frightened that one day she would eat me,' he said. 'So I made things to show her, to take her mind off it.'

He learned to draw by studying animals and their anatomy. The slaughterhouse gave him unlimited material: the thing about dead animals was that they stayed still long enough for you to draw them. His father looked carefully at all his drawings and gave him advice.

'I've often thought it's fathers who make painters,' he said, 'while writers come from their mothers.'

I asked him why he thought that.

'Mothers are such liars,' he said. 'Language is all they have. They fill you up with language if you let them.'

He had thought about taking up writing himself a few times over the years. He thought he might be able to make continuity that way, writing down the things he remembered and joining them together. But all that happened was that he realised how little he had remembered about any of it. Or maybe it was just that he didn't enjoy remembering as much as he thought he would. He never saw any member of his family again, Jeffers, after his father died and he ran away from home. Occasionally he was casually adopted by other families for a period. These were generally positive experiences, and I suppose they taught him to value choice and desire over acceptance and fate.

I realised, hearing him talk, that he was without any fibre of morality or duty, not out of any conscious decision but more in the way of lacking an elemental sense. He simply couldn't conceive of the notion of obligation. More than anything, this was what drew me to him, even as it dictated that he himself could not be drawn and even though I could see clearly that only catastrophe could come from it. I suppose he allowed me to realise the extent to which I had let my own life be defined by others. Do such people have, in fact, a higher moral function, which is to show us what our own assumptions and beliefs are made of? To put it another way, does the purpose of art extend to the artist himself as a living being? I believe it does, though there's a certain shame in biographical explanations, as though it's somehow weak-minded to look for the meaning of a created work in the life and character of the person who created it. But perhaps that shame is merely the evidence of a more general cultural condition of denial or repression, with which the artist himself is very often tempted to become complicit. I believe L had succeeded somehow in avoiding that temptation, and felt no need to dissociate himself from his own creations or claim that they were anything other than the product of a personal vision. Yet he himself, at that time, had evidently met an obstacle that he was unable to overcome. There was something, as he had said, that he had missed. But how would he ever find it, incomplete as he was?

'Why do you play at being a woman?' he asked me suddenly, with a slightly idiotic grin.

I didn't object to being asked that question, because it struck me as correct that it was what I did. What I didn't like was a joke being made out of it.

'I don't know,' I said. 'I don't think I know how to be a woman. I believe that no one ever showed me.'

'It isn't a question of showing,' he said. 'It's a question of being permitted.'

'You said when we first spoke that you couldn't see me,' I said. 'So maybe you're the one who isn't permitting.'

'You always try to force things,' he said. 'It's as if you think nothing would ever happen, unless you made it.'

'I believe nothing would,' I said.

'No one has ever broken your will.' He took his eyes off me and looked around musingly at the room. 'Who pays for all this?' he asked.

'The house and the land belong to Tony. I have some money of my own.'

'I can't imagine your little books make all that much.'

This was the first time, Jeffers, that he had alluded to my own work – if it can be called that. But up until that point his refusal to know anything about me had felt like a refusal to grant my existence, and now I understood it was because he didn't like the feeling of being compelled by my will. Yet I was convinced that he needed my will, needed it to get over the obstacle in front of him and over to the other side. We needed one another!

'I came into some money a few years ago,' I told him. 'My first husband, Justine's father, had some shares he once put in my name as a kind of dodge. He forgot that he did it, and then years later, after we were divorced, the value of these shares went through the roof. He tried to get me to sign them back over to him, but the lawyer told me I didn't have to and that the money was legally mine. So I kept it.'

The light was burning again in L's eyes.

'Was it a lot?' he said.

'On the scales of justice,' I said, 'it more or less equalled what he owed me.'

L gave a kind of hoot.

'Justice,' he said. 'What a quaint notion.'

It had felt more like an ending than a levelling, I told him, the end of an exhausting race. My little books, as he called them, had indeed made hardly any money, partly because they presented themselves to me so infrequently, and only when life had taken an ethical shape by which I had to be thoroughly broken down before I could assume that shape myself in words. I had done every kind of job in between, and lived off nerves and adrenalin, and now the greatest vice I could think of was to do nothing at all.

'I've never had enough fun,' I said to him. 'I've had other things, but never that. Perhaps it's as you say, that I force things to happen, and it's in the nature of fun not to be forced.'

When I said that, what did he do but suddenly spring to his feet and to my very great surprise leap onto the tabletop like a cat!

'Shall we have fun?' he said, cavorting there like a blazing-faced devil while I sat dumbfounded and watched him. He shouted my name over and over, stamping his feet on the table. 'Let's have some fun, shall we? Let's have some fun!'

I really can't recall, Jeffers, how I took my leave of him that day, but I do remember walking back down through the glade with a feeling that was like a wound in my chest, the way a wound is both weight and light, is fresh but fatal. I thought then of what Tony had said about L, and wondered how it was that Tony always seemed to know far more about the way things really were than anyone else.

Kurt announced that he had decided to be a writer. He wished to begin writing a book straight away. He had once heard a writer say that writing with a pen and paper was preferable to any other way, because the muscular movement of the hand was conducive to the formation of sentences. Kurt had decided that he would follow that advice. He asked for a number of pens and two big blocks of plain paper to be bought, the next time anyone went to town. I said he could use the little downstairs study if he wanted, since it was quiet and no one else needed it. It had a good-sized desk that faced away from the window – I believed most writers agreed, I said, that it was better not to have anything to look at.

As a choice of costume for his new career, Kurt decided on a long black velvet housecoat, a red tam-o'-shanter jammed far back on his head, and to top it off, rope-soled espadrilles on his bare feet. He walked fatefully off to the study in those espadrilles, carrying a block of paper under each arm and the pens in the pocket of the housecoat, and closed the door. Later, walking past the window, I saw that he had moved the desk to face the garden and the glade, so that he could see, and be seen by, everyone who passed. He was there in the window when you went out, and he was there when you came back in again. He wore a very doleful expression, looking into the far distance, and appeared not to know you if you happened to meet his eye. I wondered whether part of his intention – far from hiding himself away – was to attract attention, specifically Justine's, while at the same time keeping her under surveillance, since she was now spending a lot of her time outdoors with Brett. They did all sorts of things together, exercises, watercolour painting, even archery, using a beautiful old wooden bow Brett had apparently found in the junk shop in town and had repaired and polished up, and since the weather continued to be windless and warm they did most of it outside on the lawn or in the shade of the trees in the glade, all beneath the baleful gaze of Kurt. A few times they took Tony's boat out for the day, while Kurt remained at his window, though they had invited him to go with them. He had become a sort of icon fixed in a frame, reproaching us all for our triviality and wasted time.

By spending most of the day in the study, Kurt had effectively declared himself occupied with matters of a higher order than fence-mending or mowing, and so his affiliation to Tony quickly receded. It was now L he appeared to identify as his natural ally. I sometimes saw them in the early evening, walking in the glade and talking, though I don't know how these conversations had come about or who had initiated them. I heard Kurt say to

Justine that he and L had discussed their respective crafts, and I was quite surprised to hear it, since it was difficult to talk straight with L on any subject in an ordinary way, let alone his work. Tony didn't care that Kurt no longer followed him around: what he couldn't stand was the idea of him having nothing to do.

In a way I admired Kurt's change of direction, since at least it was some sort of constructive response to the change in Justine and to her unwillingness to content herself with playing the little wife any longer. Who knew, perhaps he was writing a masterpiece! Justine asked me, shyly, if I thought that was the case. I told her it was impossible to tell from the outside. Some of the most interesting writers could pass as bank managers, I said, while the wittiest raconteur could become dull once he had recognised the necessity of explaining his anecdotes piece by piece. Some people write simply because they don't know how to live in the moment, I said, and have to reconstruct it and live in it afterwards.

'At least he's sticking to it,' I said.

'He's used up one whole block of paper already,' she said. 'He asked me to get him some more in town.'

I was concerned about Justine's future, and something in her recent blossoming and her growing independence tore at my heartstrings – it almost felt like the less I had to worry about, the sadder I became. She had applied to do a further course of study at university in the autumn, and been accepted. She didn't say whether Kurt would be going with her – it didn't seem to be one of her considerations.

'She's starting to go out there,' Tony said to me, when I confessed these feelings to him in bed at night. He was pointing at the dark window, by which I understood him to mean the wider world.

'Oh Tony,' I said, 'it's as if I *wanted* her to get married to Kurt and spend the rest of her life dowdily waiting on him and being held back by him!'

'You want her to be safe,' Tony said, and that was exactly right: by revealing her true beauty and potential, she was somehow less safe than she had been before. I couldn't bear the thought of the hopes and possibilities that might come from this revelation, and what their crushing might do to her. Safer to go around in a Mother Hubbard, not risking anything!

'She's safer out there,' Tony said, still pointing at the window. 'As long as she has your love. You should practise giving it to her.'

He meant give it to her as something belonging to her, that she was free to take away. What was the significance of this gift? The truth was that I questioned the value of my love – I wasn't sure how much benefit it could be to anybody. I loved Justine as it were self-critically: I was working, somehow, to free her from myself, when it appeared that what she needed was to take some of me along with her!

I realised, once I thought about it, that my main principle in bringing up my daughter had been simply to do the opposite with respect to her of what had been done to me. I was good at finding those opposites and at recognising where I needed to turn left instead of right, and my moral compass had frequently led me past scenes from my own childhood that filled me with frank amazement, now that I was visiting them in reverse. But there are some things that don't really have an opposite – they need to come out of nowhere. This is perhaps the limit of honesty, Jeffers, this place where something new has to be created that bears no relation to what was there before, and it was a place I often found myself flailing in with Justine. The quality that I felt I lacked was authority, and it's difficult to say quite what the opposite of authority is because almost everything seems to be its opposite. I've often wondered about where authority comes from, whether it's the result of knowledge or character – whether, in other words, it can be learned. People know it when they see it, yet they still might not be able to say exactly what it's composed of or how it operates. When Tony said that I didn't know my own power, in fact he might have been saying something about authority and its role in shaping and cultivating power. Only tyrants want power for its own sake, and parenthood is the closest most people get to an opportunity for tyranny. Was I a tyrant, wielding shapeless power without authority? What I felt a lot of the time was a sort of stage fright, the way I imagine inexperienced teachers must feel when they stand at the front of the class looking at a sea of expectant faces. Justine had often looked at me in just that way, as though expecting an explanation for everything, and afterwards I felt I had never explained anything quite to her satisfaction, or mine.

In the past she had bristled and fought me off like a porcupine putting out her quills when I tried to show her physical affection, and so I had got into the habit of not touching her terribly often, in the end forgetting which of us this undemonstrative behaviour belonged to. I decided to begin there in any case, with the physical approach, in my practise of giving love. In the kitchen the morning after my conversation with Tony I went to her and put my arms around her, and for a while it was like hugging a small tree that doesn't move or respond but is nonetheless willing to be hugged – pleasant, but with no particular structure or sense of time. The important thing was that she didn't seem all that taken aback and she let me do it long enough for me to understand that it was something I was entitled to do. When she had decided the hug was over, she gave a little laugh and stepped back and said:

'Shall we get a dog?'

Justine often asked me why Tony and I didn't get a dog, since our life was ideally suited to having one and since she knew Tony had always had dogs before he met me. He kept a photograph of his favourite, a brown spaniel called Fetch, beside our bed. The truth was, Jeffers, I feared that if Tony got a dog, it would become the centre of his attention, and he would give it friendship and affection that should have come to me. I was in a sense in competition with this theoretical pet, many of whose characteristics – loyalty, devotion, obedience – I believed I already demonstrated. Yet I knew that Tony did in fact yearn for a dog, and that whatever he got from me, he did not confuse it in his mind with the rewards and responsibilities of animal ownership. I took this to mean that he was not entirely convinced of my loyalty or obedience, and perhaps even that a part of him would find it easier to fondle a dog than a grown woman, and only his stating that he personally did not any longer desire a dog would have persuaded me otherwise. But he had no intention of stating such a thing – all he knew, or would confess to knowing, was that I wouldn't like it, and for him the subject was therefore closed.

If I were a psychologist, I would say that this non-dog had come to stand for the concept of security, and its reappearance at the scene of my hug with Justine seemed to confirm that surmise. I mention this because it illustrates how in matters of being and becoming, an object can remain itself even at the mercy of conflicting perspectives. The non-dog represented the necessity for trusting and finding security in human beings: I preferred it that way, but Tony and Justine only had to get a sniff of that proposition to take fright. Yet the non-dog was a fact, at least for Tony and for me, and we were able to agree on it, even while it meant different things to each of us. The fact represented the boundary or separation between us, and between any two people, that it is forbidden to cross. This is very easy for someone like Tony, and very difficult for someone like me, who has trouble recognising and respecting such boundaries. I need to get at the truth of a thing and dig and dig until it is dragged painfully to light – another doglike quality. Instead all I could do was suspect, from my side of the boundary, that the two chief recipients of my love – Tony and Justine – both privately yearned for something mute and uncritical to love them instead.

Justine is very musical, and she often sang to us in the evenings and played her guitar, while we sat around the fire. She has a very sweet voice and a wistful, penetrating air when she sings that I have always found affecting. She had been practising a song with Brett, for which she had written a harmony, and they decided to perform it for us one evening at the house after dinner. Kurt then announced that he would like to use the occasion to read from his work in progress. Tony and I bustled around tidying things and arranging chairs and setting out drinks, for I had a sense that L might attend this cultural soirée and I wanted the house to look welcoming, even while his remarks about my playing at being a woman were ringing in my ears. I was beginning to understand that L had a way of making you see yourself without being able to do terribly much about what you saw. While I went on with the preparations I imagined being a different kind of person, someone careless and selfish who was confident that those same qualities would produce a successful evening. How I wished, sometimes, to be that person!

At the appointed hour I saw through the window that my guess had been right, and that two figures were approaching through the glade. Brett came in wearing a startling little dress, a kind of slip or negligee that showed more of her than it covered, and this revelation of flesh instantly created an atmosphere of awkwardness, since it seemed to be part of something private that was happening between her and L. Brett's face was flushed and her strange letterbox mouth hung blackly open. Her expression had a certain wildness, and I began to feel the blankness and dread that always overcome me in the presence of social tension. There was a wild light in L's eyes too, and every now and then the two of them would look at one another and laugh.

We sat around and talked for a while. I don't know what we talked about – I never do, in a situation like that. Tony imperturbably made drinks for people and acted as though nothing was wrong. Brett downed two cocktails one after the other, which seemed to have the curious effect of sobering her up. L accepted one drink, which he placed fastidiously on a side table and didn't look at again. I glanced frequently over at Justine, who was sitting in a low chair beside the fire with her guitar laid flat across her knees and a meditative expression on her face, even while Brett kept bursting out into shrill laughter next to her. At a certain point she picked up her guitar and began to play softly, and then to hum to herself. L, as usual, had sat as far away from me as he could get, and Kurt was beside him. The two of them were talking, or rather L was talking and Kurt was listening: L had turned his head and was speaking straight into Kurt's ear, which I suppose he had to do as his voice was so indistinct and there were other noises in the room. Justine's playing eventually started to have a calming effect, on Brett as well as on Tony and me, and when she began to sing in her sweet voice we fell quiet and listened. Kurt, too, turned his head toward Justine, so that L had to change position to keep talking in his ear. After a while Kurt turned away from her again to listen to L, but he kept glancing back at her with a strange, cold expression in his eyes, and I saw then that his loyalties had somehow become divided, and I sensed L was to blame for it.

The song Justine was playing was a familiar song, and we began to sing along with it, as we often did in that situation. These times were very dear to me, Jeffers, because I always felt deep down that it was me Justine was singing for, and that her song was the song of our wanderings together through time, from her first day of life to the present moment. And in this particular moment I admired her more than ever, since she seemed to have disclosed a new power in bringing righteous order back to our situation. Brett had pulled a coat on over her slip and sang along in a husky, pleasant kind of voice, and Tony struck chords with his strong, low voice, and I matched my singing to Justine's as best I could. Even Kurt joined in eventually, if only out of habit. The only person who wasn't singing was L, and I didn't believe for a minute that this was because he didn't know how to sing or didn't know the tune. He *wouldn't* sing, and the reason he wouldn't was because everyone else was singing and it was in his nature not to be coerced. Another person might at least have gone to the trouble to appear charmed or entertained by the scene, but L merely sat there with a weary look on his face, as though he were using this as an opportunity to think about all the other tiresome things he had been made to sit through. Sometimes he would look up and meet my eye, and something of his separation would become my own. The strangest feeling of detachment, almost of disloyalty, would come over me: even there, in the midst of the things I loved best, he had the ability to cast me into doubt and to expose in myself what was otherwise shrouded over. It was as though, in those moments, his terrible objectivity became my own and I saw things the way they really are.

It almost goes without saying, Jeffers, that part of L's greatness lay in his ability to be right about the things that he saw, and what confounded me was how, at the plane of living, this rightness could be so discordant and cruel. Or rather, what was so liberating and rewarding in looking at a painting by L became acutely uncomfortable when one encountered or lived it in the flesh. It was the feeling that there could be no excuses or explanations, no dissimulating: he filled one with the dreadful suspicion that there is no story to life, no personal meaning beyond the meaning of any given moment. Something in me loved this feeling, or at the very least knew it and recognised it to be true, as one must recognise darkness and acknowledge its truth alongside that of light; and in that same sense I knew and recognised L. I haven't loved very many people in my life – before Tony, I never really loved anyone. I was only now learning to love Justine with something other than the usual mother-love and to see her as she actually was. True love is the product of freedom, and I'm not sure a parent and child can ever have that kind of love, unless they decide to start over again as adults. I loved Tony and I loved Justine and I loved L, Jeffers, even though the time I spent with him was so often bitter and painful, because he drew me with the cruelty of his rightness closer to the truth.

Brett and Justine sang their song together very charmingly, and then they sang it again since I begged them to, and when that was over Kurt stood up in his black velvet housecoat and came to stand in front of us beside the fire-place to read. He had a block of pages an inch thick which he placed solemnly on a table beside him, and he began to read without introduction, in a loud and doleful voice, lifting one page after another from the top of the block and afterwards placing them facedown on the other side, until we realised he must be intending to read the whole thing! We all sat without moving or speaking, a captive audience, as this knowledge dawned on us – I couldn't understand how he had managed to produce so much writing in so little time. It was set in an alternate world, Jeffers, with dragons and monsters and armies of imaginary creatures interminably fighting one another, and great lists of names like in parts of the Old Testament, and pages of oracular-sounding dialogue which Kurt spoke out very slowly and solemnly. After an hour or so of this I sort of came to and began to look around out of the corner of my eye. The fire had gone out, and Tony was asleep in his chair, while Brett and Justine sat with glazed faces, their heads leaning together. Only L appeared to be paying attention: he sat very still in his chair with his hands folded in his lap and his head cocked slightly to the side. Finally, after nearly two hours, Kurt had read his way through the whole block and he laid down the last page, heaving a great sigh with his arms hanging by his sides and his head thrown back, while we roused ourselves to applaud.

'That's it so far,' he gasped. 'What do you think?'

It was one o'clock in the morning by then, and whether or not any of us had anything to say, I for one was reluctant to prolong the evening much further! I tried to think of a comment to make for politeness's sake, but I wasn't sure I remembered anything at all about what he'd read. I expected Justine at least to contribute something, but she just sat with Brett's head on her shoulder and an air of abstraction, as though whatever it was she might have said couldn't be uttered out loud. Tony had opened his eyes, but that was all. L appeared quite composed, remaining very erect and wide-awake in his chair, with his fingers laced beneath his chin. The silence extended until I felt sure it would snap, and just before that happened L spoke.

'It's really far too long,' he said, in his quiet, unhurried voice.

I guessed that Kurt had never once considered length to be a matter of concern in the production of literature – on the contrary, he had probably taken it as a sign that things were going well!

'It has to be,' he said, rather stiffly.

'But it's over now,' L said. 'So why does it? Why does it have to take up time?'

'It's how the story goes,' Kurt said. He looked rather confused. 'That was only the first section.'

L lifted his eyebrows and gave a small smile.

'But my time belongs to me,' he said. 'Be careful what you ask people to endure.'

And with that he calmly stood up and bid us all goodnight and vanished into the darkness! For a few moments Kurt just stood there, white-faced and stricken. Justine stirred herself and embarked on some propitiatory comment or other, but he put up a hand to silence her. He began to cast terrible glances around the room, as though it were full of enemy assailants closing in on him. Then he grabbed the sheaf of paper and tucked it under his arm and bolted out into the darkness too! Justine told me later that Kurt's novel was in fact quite a faithful copy of a book the two of them had read a few months earlier: she believed he hadn't really been aware of what he was doing, and that when the ideas had come into his head he had thought he was imagining them himself rather than simply remembering them. The next day he was no longer to be seen in the study window. He appeared in the kitchen wearing his normal clothes, and kept at a distance from everybody. I saw him wandering forlornly in the garden and I went out to find him, since I felt sorry for him by this point and wondered whether I should have done more to look after him. How guilty a man like that can make you feel, Jeffers! The truth was that in another compartment of my mind I was considering making him disappear altogether by marching him down to the train station, buying him a ticket and sending him straight back to the bosom of his ideal family; and my guilt-reaction sat across from this impulse and the two of them stared at one another gloomily.

'It's all that man's fault,' he surprised me by saying, when I discovered him sitting perched on a rock by the stream that runs through the orchard, like an oversized garden gnome. I asked him if he meant L, and he nodded miserably. 'He gave me all kinds of strange advice.'

'What did he tell you?' I said.

'He told me to stop being such a – such a *milquetoast*,' Kurt said. 'That was the word he used. I didn't know what it meant but I looked it up. He told me if I wanted to improve things with Justine I needed to find a mistress, and that the best mistress of all was work. It was because I admitted to him that I thought Justine didn't love me any more,' he said. 'That's how it started. He said I should try writing, because it was cheap and you didn't need any particular talent.'

'What else did he say?'

'He said that I should never let Justine know what I was thinking. He said that if Justine was nice to me then I could be nice back. But if she wasn't nice, I should break her. He said I had to break her will, and that the way to do it was to always do the opposite of what she expected or wanted me to do. He's a terrible man.' Kurt was looking at me in wide-eyed terror. 'He says he intends to destroy you.'

'Destroy me?'

'That's what he says. But I won't let him destroy you!'

Well, I didn't know where to begin with this outburst, except that I did recognise the part about breaking people's wills. The thing was, Jeffers, part of me wanted to be destroyed, even as I feared that a whole reality would collapse along with it, the reality shared by other people and things – the whole web of deeds and associations that contained both past and future and was clogged with all the evidence of the great dirty passage of time, yet always failed somehow to capture the living moment. What I wanted to get rid of was the part of me that had always been there, and I believe that this was the essence of the feeling I shared with L, as he himself had explained it in our first conversation. There was a greater reality, I believed, beyond or behind or beneath the reality I knew, and it seemed to me that a lifelong pain would be ended if only I could break through to it. It didn't seem to me any longer that this was something you could think your way into – the psychoanalyst had carried that idea away with him, when he ran off down the street. It needed violence, the actual destruction of the ailing part, just as the body sometimes needs surgery to cure it. It seemed to me that this was the form freedom took out of necessity, the final form, when every other attempt to attain it had failed. I didn't know what this violence was or how it could be inflicted, only that something in L's threat seemed to promise it.

I asked Kurt whether he thought he would like to go home for a while, and if so whether he would like me to help him arrange it.

'I can't leave you,' Kurt said. 'It would be too dangerous.'

I assured him that I would be perfectly fine, and that if necessary I had Tony to protect me, but he was adamant that he had to remain in order to avert the possibility of my destruction. Later that day Justine came to me full of indignation, asking why I was trying to send Kurt home behind her back. I tried to defend myself, and one way or another the little structure of love we had been building together was knocked down and would have to be built all over again.

After I met Tony for the first time, he wrote to me nearly every day for a month or more, until circumstances allowed me to come and meet him again, since at that time I was living some distance away. I was very surprised by his letters, which were extremely well written and poetic, and also by the regularity with which they came. It was as if he were beating a drum, steadily and without cease, that I heard across all the miles that separated us until I recognised that it was summoning me. Tony's letters gave me the first experience I had ever had of satisfaction – of my most secret hopes and desires, and my sense of life's possibility, being met. They were always prompter and more numerous and longer and more beautiful than I expected, and they never disappointed me. Whatever I imagined getting from Tony, it wasn't this sparkling river of words that flowed through me and irrigated me and began to bring me slowly back to life. It has allowed me ever after to live with his silence, because I know that the river is there, and that only I am permitted to have this knowledge.

During those strange weeks with L, I thought often

back to Tony's letters and to the time when our love began. Though it was only a matter of months, that time was so large and luminous that it dwarfed entire decades of my life, like a great edifice in the middle of a city that can be seen from miles away. In a sense its abundance took it outside of time altogether, and by that I mean that it's still there: I can visit it and live in it for hours, and part of the reason I can is that it is built on a foundation of language. I'm making another building here, Jeffers, out of the time I spent with L, but I'm not sure quite what kind of a building it is, nor whether I will ever be able to come back to visit it. There's a certain point in life at which you realise it's no longer interesting that time goes forward – or rather, that its forward-going-ness has been the central plank of life's illusion, and that while you were waiting to see what was going to happen next, you were steadily being robbed of all you had. Language is the only thing capable of stopping the flow of time, because it exists in time, is made of time, yet it is eternal – or can be. An image is also eternal, but it has no dealings with time – it disowns it, as it has to do, for how could one ever in the practical world scrutinise or comprehend the balance sheet of time that brought about the image's unending moment? Yet the spirituality of the image beckons us, as our own sight does, with the promise to free us from ourselves. In the midst of the practical reality of my life with Tony, I felt the lure of abundance again, emanating from L – yet where Tony's language had flowed toward and into me, L's call was the reverse. It was the inchoate call out of some mystery or void.

That call had grown very faint as the days passed, and just as I had started to believe that I could no longer hear it at all and that L had become once more a stranger to me, I met him unexpectedly out walking on the marsh. I was down there collecting leaves from some of the edible sea plants that grow around the creeks, to cook them for dinner – I am always quite proud of this activity, Jeffers, which sometimes feels like the only proper use I ever make of myself – and he came around a bend in the path. He was more casually dressed than usual, and his face was quite ruddy from the sun, and altogether he looked more human and less of a devil than he generally did. His trousers were rolled up and he carried his shoes in his hand, and he told me he had gone out to one of the sandbars while the tide was coming in and had had to wade back!

'And then,' he said, quite breathlessly, and seeming to find it all rather exciting, 'as I was walking back up, I heard people shooting. I looked around for a while but I couldn't see anyone. The shots seemed to be coming one at a time from different places. I was thinking, first I nearly drown, then I have to face down a gunman, or several of them. Is there someone I should tell?'

As he spoke, the sound of a single loud report rang into the air from the field behind him and he flinched.

'There it is again,' he said.

I told him it was only one of the stationary gas guns the farmers put in their fields at that time of year to keep the birds off their crops. I was used to the sound and was barely startled by it, and in that half-conscious state I could hear it as all kinds of things. Sometimes I liked to imagine, I told him, that it was the sound of wicked men blowing their brains out, one after another.

'Huh,' he said, with a grudging half-smile. 'Wicked men don't do that. Anyway, you'd probably like those men if you got to know them. Nothing evil ever dies. Especially not of remorse.'

His calves were streaked with mud up to the knee, and I told him he needed to be careful of the tides, which were dangerous if you didn't know where the paths were.

'I was trying to find the edge,' he said, looking away from me toward where the horizon lay smudged and indistinct in haze, 'but there is no edge. You just get worn down by the slow curvature. I wanted to see what here looks like from there. I walked a long way out, but there *is* no there – it just sort of dissolves, doesn't it? There are no lines here at all.'

I waited in silence for him to say something more, and after the longest time he resumed:

'You know, a lot of people get a bad idea right around when they've just passed the middle of their lives. They see a kind of mirage and they go into another building phase, but in fact they're building death. That's maybe what happened to me after all. I suddenly saw it, right out there,' he said, pointing toward the distant blue shape of the receded tide, 'the illusion of that death-structure. I wish I had understood before how to dissolve. Not just how to dissolve the line – other things too. I did the opposite, because I thought I had to resist being worn down. The more I tried to make a structure, the more it felt like everything around me had gone bad. It felt like I was making the world, and making it wrong, when all I was doing was making my own death. But you don't have to die. The dissolving looks like death but in fact it's the other way around. I didn't see it to start with.'

When L said these things, Jeffers, I felt a thrill of vindication – I *knew* he would understand it! It was a grey, windy morning, and the marsh looked at its least mysterious in that ordinary, glaring light. It appeared somehow technical, and it was that same technical matter-of-factness that gladdened my heart, because it reassured me that L and I were looking at the same thing. I have seen it at such pitches of the sublime – in certain moods and lights and weathers – that it has wrung every emotion out of me, but in its plainest colours, as it was that morning, its reality is indubitable. As far as I knew, he hadn't by that point made any work about the marsh – but he did say that his portrait phase had just about run its course. The trouble was, he said, there weren't enough people around, other than working people who were too busy to sit for him. He didn't know why he hadn't realised that at the start. He had painted Tony, and Justine, and Kurt, and so he'd just about run through the repertoire, unless he could go into town and kidnap some more subjects.

'I wondered about painting people who aren't here any more,' he said. 'The thought of it makes me sick. But if I could get over the sickness . . .'

I reminded him that there was one human subject here that he hadn't yet attempted – me! He had said before that he couldn't see me, and he had never explained why he couldn't, and I was well aware that he avoided physical proximity to me at every opportunity. In romantic stories, avoidance of one person by another is often used as a device in the plot of love, the implication being that certain natures betray what they desire by appearing to disdain it. What hopeful and tragic fantasies the authors of those plots shamelessly play on! I didn't delude myself that L was suppressing an attraction to me, but I did think it was curious that I represented such an obstacle to him. Almost, I wondered whether the removal of that obstacle might help him move forward, which is why I had no particular shame about suggesting he put me in a frame, the way he'd done to Tony. Kurt's mention, that day in the garden, of L's wish to destroy me had reinforced that impression. Why shouldn't he just come out and say why he thought I ought to be destroyed?

He didn't reply straight away to my remark, but stood for a while with his arms folded tight and his face turned into the wind and into the hard, flat light, as though he found the discomfort consoling. Painting people, he said eventually, was an act of both scrutiny and idolatry in which – for him, at least – the coldness of separation had to be maintained at all costs. For this reason he had always been especially disturbed by artists who painted their children. When people fall in love, he said, they experience this coldness as the greatest frisson of all, the fascination of a subject that can still be seen as distinct from oneself. The more familiar the loved one becomes, the less that frisson can be obtained. Worship, in other words, comes before knowledge, and in life this represents the complete initial loss or abandonment of objectivity, followed by a good long dose of reality while the truth is revealed. A portrait is more like an act of promiscuity, he said, in which coldness and desire coexist to the end, and it requires a certain hard-heartedness, which was why he had thought it was the right direction for him to take at this moment. Whatever promiscuity he had indulged in in his younger years, he had been fooling himself, because the hardening of his heart with age was of a different magnitude. The quality that attracted him now was unavailability, the deep moral unavailability of certain people, so that to have them was in effect to steal them and violate – or at least experience – their untouchability. Disgust came easily to him these days, he was filled to the brim with it, so it didn't take much to make him overflow, and he wondered sometimes whether this was the presentation at long last of the bill for his childhood, when he had held his disgust inside himself year after year. Whatever the reason, he said, that quality of untouchability was the antidote to it, to the sickness that overcame him whenever he caught the stench of human familiarity.

While he spoke, a feeling had been growing inside me, of the most abject rejection and abandonment, because what I understood him to be saying underneath all his explanations was that my used-up female body was disgusting to him, and that this was the reason he kept me at a distance, even to the point of being unable to sit next to me!

'It may come as a surprise to you to hear it, but I'm also trying to find a way of dissolving,' I said to him indignantly, while tears surged in my eyes. 'That's why I wanted you to come here. You're not the only one who feels that way. You can't just blot me out, because it makes you feel sick to see me – I'm just as untouchable as anyone else! I don't exist to be seen by you,' I said, 'so don't delude yourself on that point, because I'm the one that's trying to free myself from how you see me. You'd feel better if you could see what I actually am, but you can't. Your sight is a kind of murder, and I won't be murdered any more.'

And I put my face in my hands and wept!

Well, what I learned that morning was that however wicked and terrible an artist permits himself to become on the human scale, somewhere inside him there is a part that remains capable of pity – or rather, when that part is gone, so is his art. The truest test of a person is the test of compassion. Is that true, Jeffers? In any event, L was very kind to me that morning, and he even put his arms around me and let me weep on his chest while he stroked my hair, and he said:

'There, there, honey. Don't cry,' in a soft, kind voice which made me cry even harder.

The feeling of physical closeness to him was quite disturbing to me, as it had come to seem somehow forbidden that we should ever touch, even by accident. I didn't quite like being touched by him. It made the question of disgust, which I had tried to stamp down, rise up again, except that this time it felt as though it was I who was disgusted by him. Perhaps it's the case that L had – and who knows, maybe all men have – only one way of touching a woman, in which their automatic selves are set into involuntary motion. I didn't want that automatic, shop-soiled touching. I disentangled myself from him as soon as I could, and sat down on the grass and put my head on my knees and wept some more. After a while L sat down beside me, and in the silence the soothing sights and sounds of the marsh, the waving grasses flecked with butterflies, the distant soughing of the sea, the trailing ribbons of birdsong and the calls of the geese and gulls, could come into focus.

'It's good to sit and watch this gentle world,' L said. 'We tire ourselves out so.'

Sitting there I began to tell him about the time all those years before when I had walked through a Paris morning in the sun and come upon rooms full of his paintings, and about how it had made me feel, to experience the sort of kinship those images had aroused in me, as though I had suddenly discovered my true origins. They had made me feel that I was not alone in what, until then, I had held as secret to myself. The admission of that secret there in his work, I said, had led to a change in my life's orientation, because suddenly the secret felt stronger than the things that had kept it hidden. But this change of course had been much more effortful and violent than I could have foreseen, and it had looked at times as though I had entered on the path to disaster, and what I couldn't understand was how the simple revelation of personal truth could lead to so much suffering and cruelty, when surely it was morally inoffensive to seek to live in a condition of truth.

I had learned since then, I said, that I was naive to expect that other people would merely allow me to change when those changes directly interfered with their own interests, and the revelation that my whole life, which appeared to have been built on love and freedom of choice, was in fact a facade that concealed the most craven selfishness was deeply shocking to me. There is no limit, I said, to what certain people will do to you if you offend them or take away what they want, and the fact that at one time you liked or chose to be among those people is one of the central mysteries and tragedies of life. Yet it is only a reflection, I said, of the very conditions and substances out of which your humanity is made – it is the attempt by selfishness and dishonesty to reproduce themselves in you and to continue to flourish in the world. You might as well go mad, I said, as try to resist that attempt.

'Did you go mad?' L asked.

'I didn't go mad,' I said. 'Though I suppose I still might, one day.'

I told him about how automatically I had believed – or rather, had assumed – that Justine's father was a nice, or at least a decent man. How easy it is, Jeffers, to believe that of the men who conform to our idea of normality! I don't think a woman is ever taken on trust in that way, unless it's through the notion of her subservience. Yet within less than a month of my return from Paris and my announcement that I wanted to change the way things were, I had lost my home, my money, my friends, and even then I didn't foresee the greater losses that were ahead of me. Justine was four years old at that time, and capable of expressing an opinion, and one day when she was at his house – as it now was – her father called me to say that she didn't want me to collect her, as had been arranged. He even put her on the phone, so I could hear her say it myself. It was a year, Jeffers, before I got her back, and during that year I would often go and hide like a wraith at the gates of her school in the hope of catching a glimpse of her, until one day he happened to see me when he was coming out hand in hand with her, and he pointed at me and said to her:

'There's that terrible woman – run, Justine, run!'

And the two of them ran away down the street! That was when I tried to make myself die, but I couldn't die – mothers can't, really, unless it happens by accident. I discovered afterwards that he had been terribly neglectful of her all through this period, and often left her alone for hours on end, as though he had retained this part of me specifically so that he could demonstrate his cruelty and indifference toward it. This was my sorrow, Jeffers, and I gave it to L sitting there on the marsh, through fits of weeping. What I wanted L to understand was that this will of mine that he so objected to had survived numerous attempts to break it, and at this point could be credited with my own survival and that of my child. It had likewise brought disaster and dispossession on me – but better dispossession than to live where hatred walks around disguised as love! To lose my will would be to lose my hold on life – to go mad – and I was in no doubt that it could break one day of its own accord, I said to L, but it was my suspicion that a woman's madness represents the final refuge of the male secret, the place where he would destroy her rather than be revealed, and I had no intention now of being destroyed in that way – I would sooner destroy my-self, I said, if Justine was capable of understanding my reasons for doing it. What I wanted instead was for L to meet me on the basis of that recognition I had felt that day in Paris – I wanted to be recognised by him, because grateful as I was for Tony and Justine and for my existence at the marsh, my individuality had tormented me my whole life with its demand to be recognised.

'All right,' he said quietly, after a long silence. 'Come across later and let me look at you. Wear something that fits,' he added.

Well, Jeffers, I grabbed my bag of sea leaves and I leaped to my feet and I ran back up to the house in a state of pure joy – I felt all at once so light and unburdened, I thought I might just fly up to the sun! Everything seemed transformed, the day, the landscape, the meaning of my presence in it, as if it had been turned inside out. I was like a person who walks for the first time without pain, after a long, long illness. I ran up the lawn and along the flower beds and as I came around the corner to the house I bumped into Tony.

'Isn't it a wonderful day?' I said to him. 'Isn't everything just wonderful?'

He gave me a lengthy and very beady look.

'Looks like you need to go and lie down for a while,' he said.

'But Tony, don't be ridiculous – I'm full of energy!' I cried. 'I feel like I could build a house or chop down a whole forest or – '

I couldn't keep still any longer and I ran into the house

and through the kitchen, where Justine and Kurt were standing quietly at the counter, shelling the mountain of peas that had just come in from the garden.

'Isn't it beautiful outside?' I said. 'I feel so alive today!'

They both lifted their faces and stared dumbly at me and I left my bag of leaves on the counter and ran on, up the stairs and into my room, and I closed the door behind me and dropped down on the bed. Why didn't anyone want me to be happy? Why were they all so disapproving, the minute I showed any excitement and high spirits? My mood began to deflate a little with these thoughts. I sat there on the bed and went back over my conversation with L, and thought again about the feeling his attention had given me, which was a golden feeling of health. Oh, why was living so painful, and why were we given these moments of health, if only to realise how burdened with pain we were the rest of the time? Why was it so difficult to live day after day with people and still remember that you were distinct from them and that this was your one mortal life?

After all I found that Tony was right, and that I did need to lie down quietly, and I lay there and breathed and savoured the marvellous feeling of lightness, as though some great malevolent lump had been removed from inside me. In the end, it wasn't anyone else's business that the lump had been there, nor that it was gone – the whole point was that I had to learn to live more in myself. Everybody else, it seemed to me, lived perfectly happily in themselves. Only I drifted around like a vagrant spirit, cast out of the home of myself to be buffeted by every word and mood and whim of other people! Sensitivity all at once seemed to me like the most terrible curse, Jeffers, foraging for truth in a million pointless details, when in fact there was only one truth, and it lay beyond the power of description. There was only this lack or lightness that words fled away from, and I lay on the bed and felt it, and tried not to think too much about what it was and how one could describe it.

But we live in time – we can't help it! Eventually I had to get up and go downstairs, and there were all the usual chores to do and all the enacting of oneself that living with other people requires, and one way or another it was late afternoon before I was able to contemplate going across to the second place for my assignation with L. All through those hours and those chores I was aware that a great change had taken place in me, and I kept hoping someone else would notice it. The thought of L looking at me had made me look at myself, and because I could see myself I expected the others to see me too! But they acted as usual, even Tony, and when I slipped away upstairs to get changed it all seemed so normal that I remained convinced that what I was doing was normal as well.

I opened my cupboard of clothes and felt a sudden qualm at the prospect of trying to find what I wanted, so sure was I that what I wanted wasn't there. As I have already said, Jeffers, I had at some point given up on the attempt to learn the language of clothes, and if someone had given me a uniform I would gladly have worn it every day, but instead I had devised a sort of uniform of my own, in that everything I possessed was more or less the same. But none of it answered to L's description, which was to wear something that fitted, and as I rummaged hopelessly in the cupboard I remembered that before I came to the marsh my clothes *had* been more fitted, and that perhaps the last day on which I had worn something fitted was the day I married Tony! Thinking this made me feel suddenly tearful, and I had the awful feeling of an unravelling deep inside me. Did Tony not appreciate me as a woman with a female form? Did I go around in shapeless clothes these days as a kind of renunciation of sexuality and beauty? Clawing in the very back of the cupboard with a sudden and instinctive certainty, I found myself pulling out the very same dress I had got married in, which I had entirely forgotten was there. It was a beautiful, simple, close-fitting dress, and as I held it in my hands I knew it was exactly right, while at the same time I was beset by waves of conflicting emotion, chief among them a nameless kind of sorrow, for the people Tony and I had been then, as if those people no longer existed.

Filled with daring I put the dress on, and was arranging my hair in front of the mirror when Tony walked into the room. Tony is rarely excited or perturbed, and this occasion was no exception. I had wondered whether he might be so moved by the sight of the dress that he wouldn't notice I hadn't put it on for him, but he simply lifted his head a little and looked at me for a while and then stated:

'You're wearing your dress.'

'L has finally asked to paint me,' I said to him, all in a flutter and trying not to let him notice, 'and he told me to wear something close-fitting, and this was the only thing I could think of!'

I decided it was better not to say anything else, even though part of me was also aching to receive Tony's compliments and to sit and talk with him about the people we once were, and whether or not those people still existed. Instead, while he was digesting the information I had given him, I slipped past him and sped out through the door and down the stairs. The afternoon had become a little overcast and now, in the early evening, a kind of gloom had fallen over the glade. I wondered whether the bad light might affect my sitting with L and whether he would cancel it, and whether in fact he would be there at all, since now that I came to think of it we hadn't arranged a specific time. I let myself out of the house and scurried up the path that leads into the trees, and saw that all the lights of the second place were on, making a great glowing shape in the distance. I felt the air on my uncovered shoulders and arms, and the unaccustomed feeling of my hair falling against my bare back, and a feeling of youth and freedom surged through me as I hastened toward the glade and the distant cube of light. At that moment, I heard the clattering sound behind me of a window being opened, and I stopped and turned around and looked up. There was Tony, standing at the open window of our bedroom, looking down on me from a great height. Our eyes met, and he held out a terrible arm at me and he thundered:

'COME BACK HERE!'

For a second I stood frozen to the spot, looking up into Tony's eyes. Then I turned and ran off into the trees, skulking and shamefaced as a runaway dog. I went quickly through the glade toward the lighted windows, and since L and Brett had taken down the curtains I was able to see inside in more detail the closer I got. First I saw that the furniture had been pushed aside against the cupboards and shelves, and then I saw two figures, L and Brett, moving so strangely around the room that at first I thought they were dancing. But then, as I drew nearer, I realised they were painting – and what's more, painting on the walls of the second place!

They were both barely dressed, L with no shirt on and great blotches of paint across his naked chest, and Brett in a camisole and briefs with a scarf tied around her hair. While I watched, L wiped the back of his hand across his nose with a savage gesture and left a long streak of paint over his face too. Brett pointed at it and doubled over with laughter. They had taken the little stepladder from the shed and were using it to reach all the way to the top of the walls, which were half-covered in a growing swirl of lurid colours and shapes. I stopped and stood, rooted to the spot, unable to help seeing what I saw through the glass. I saw the forms of trees and plants and flowers, the trees with great twisting intestinal roots, the flowers fleshy and obscene, with big pink stamens like phalluses; and strange animals, birds and beasts of unearthly shapes and colours; and in the middle of it all two figures, a woman and a man, standing beside a tree bearing violent red fruits like countless open mouths, with a great fat snake wound all around its trunk. It was a Garden of Eden, Jeffers, except a hellish one! I stepped closer to the windows – I could hear harsh music, and above that the sounds of their voices, which seemed to come in bellows and shrieks and gusts

141

of shrill laughter – while the two of them moved around inside as though possessed by demonic energy, splashing and smearing paint over the walls. They were working on the Eve figure, and I heard L say:

'Let's give her a moustache, the castrating bitch!' while Brett shrieked with laughter. '*Cause* of all the trouble,' he said, blotting the figure's upper lip with thick black strokes.

'And let's give her a nice fat little belly,' Brett cried, 'a barren belly like a middle-aged lady's! She's skinny all over, but that belly gives her away, the bitch.'

'A big hairy moustache,' L said, 'so we know who's in charge. We know who's in charge, don't we? Don't we?'

And the two of them howled, while I stood in my wedding dress beyond the window in the glade where night was falling and trembled, trembled to the soles of my feet. It was me they were talking about, me they were painting – I was Eve! A terrible darkness flooded my mind, so that for a while I couldn't see or think or move. And then a thought came, and it was that I had to get back to Tony. I turned and ran back down along the path through the trees, and as I was approaching the house I saw two red lights in the driveway at the front. They glowed for a minute and then began to recede, amid the sound of an engine. I realised that it was our truck, and that Tony was inside it, and was driving away! I ran out to the driveway and stood there calling his name, but the lights disappeared around the bend and I knew that he had left me and gone, and I didn't know whether he would ever come back again.

Symbolically enough, the fine weather broke the very next day and it started to rain, and I sat and looked out of the window at the falling water without speaking or moving at all. At a certain point I heard the sound of a car at the front of the house and I bolted outside, believing that Tony had come back, but it was only one of the men, who had driven up to tell me that Tony had asked him to lend me a car, since he had gone away in the truck. Gone away! I went and sat and looked out of the window again. How sad the rain was, falling after all these weeks of warmth and sun. I thought about Tony's irrigation system, and how he had kept everything alive day after day while the rest of us had rejoiced in the fine weather, and I began to weep while it dawned on me anew how responsible and good Tony was and how frivolous and selfish were the rest of us. Sometimes Justine came and sat beside me and looked out of the window too at the rain falling, and I saw that she was nearly as sad as I was that Tony was gone. She asked me if I knew when he would be coming back, and I said that I didn't. When it got dark I went upstairs and lay on our bed and tried to talk to Tony. There in the darkness I concentrated my whole self on talking to him in my heart and hoping he would hear me, wherever he was.

The next day two more of the men came, to do Tony's outdoor chores and the various pieces of work that always need to be done on the land. I remained very still and quiet, talking to Tony in my heart, as I had been doing all night. I did not for a minute doubt his loyalty or his reasons for acting as he had done – what I doubted was myself and my ability ever to convince him that I was still the person he had believed me to be. The thing is, Jeffers, that between two people as different as Tony and me there needs to be an act almost of translation, and at times of crisis it's very easy for something to get lost in that act. How could we be sure we understood one another? How could we know that what we were seeing and responding to was the same thing? The second place was just one example of our attempts to accommodate those distinctions, because both of us realised that in a marriage like ours you couldn't always be fed from the same source. There was a freedom in that situation but there was also a kind of sorrow that came if you ever suspected it of representing a limitation in your bond to one another.

For me, Tony's differences were a test of my ability to contain my own will, which was always straining to make everything how I wanted and thought it should be, to make it conform to my idea. If Tony were to conform to my idea, he would no longer be Tony! I don't know what, in me, represented a similar test to him, and it isn't my business to know, but I remember when we were building the second place, and had come to start calling it that in a way I knew would never change if we carried on doing it much longer, I said to him that 'second place' pretty much summed up how I felt about myself and my life – that it had been a near miss, requiring just as much effort as victory but with that victory always and forever somehow denied me, by a force that I could only describe as the force of pre-eminence. I could never win, and the reason I couldn't seemed to lie within certain infallible laws of destiny that I was powerless – as the woman I was – to overcome. I ought to have accepted it at the beginning, and spared myself the effort! Tony listened to me, and I could tell he was slightly surprised by what I was saying, and that he was thinking about why he was, and after a long time he said:

'For me it doesn't mean that. It means parallel world. Alternative reality.'

Well, Jeffers, I laughed heartily to myself at this perfect example of the paradox that is Tony and me!

When we got married, I remember the minister confidentially asking me whether I would prefer the word *obey* to be excised from the marriage vows – a lot of women these days did prefer it, he said, with a sort of wink. I replied that no, I wanted to keep it there, because it seemed to me that to love someone is to be prepared to obey them, to obey even the smallest child, and that a love that makes no promise of relenting or of acquiescence is either an incomplete or a tyrannical love. Most of us are perfectly happy to give our obedience without even thinking about it to almost any tin-pot thing that sets itself up over us as an authority! I promised to obey Tony and he promised to obey me, and what I didn't know, as I sat there looking through the window at the rain, was whether this vow – as some vows are – was entirely dishonoured by being once broken. In my heart I was asking him to obey me and come back home, and it almost made me feel powerful to ask it, because by asking it I was forced to understand how he had felt that night when I ran away from him into the glade. I was asking, in other words, as a more knowledgeable person than the person I had been then, and this felt like a kind of authority, and I hoped he would hear it and recognise it.

It rained for five days straight, and the earth got darker and the grass got greener and the trees drank with their heads down and their branches bowed. The gutters once more dripped into the water butts, and everywhere you went you could hear the constant ticking sound the drops made when they fell. The marsh lay sullen in the distance, cloaked in cloud, although sometimes a bar of cold white light would appear there and frozenly burn. It was a mysterious sight, this opalescent form far, far out and all coldly alight. It did not seem to emanate from the sun, and there was a frigid godliness to it that things lit by the sun do not possess. I stayed mostly in my room, and saw no one but Justine, who sometimes came and sat with me. She asked me whether I thought Tony had left because of L.

'He left because I made him look ridiculous,' I said. 'L just happened to be the cause.'

'Brett wants to leave too,' Justine told me. 'She says L is a bad influence on her. She says he takes too many drugs, and sometimes she takes them with him and they're affecting her. I don't know how she can stand it,' she said, shuddering. 'He's so old and dried up. There's nothing he can give her. He's just a vampire on her youth.'

I felt very bad, Jeffers, hearing this description of L – it made the whole business of his presence here seem sordid, a sordidness for which I was responsible and in which I had implicated us all. I decided then and there that I would ask him to leave. There was something so small and suburban in this decision that I hated myself for it straight away. It made me unequal to L, the inferior of his own base acts, and I could easily imagine him laughing in my face for it. He could refuse, and then I would have to compel him to leave, by physical force if necessary – that was where that kind of decision got you!

I asked Justine whether she'd been over to the second place and seen what they'd done there and she looked at me guiltily.

'Are you very angry?' she said. 'It wasn't Brett's fault, not really.'

I said I wasn't especially angry – it was more that I was shocked, and shock is sometimes necessary, for without it we would drift into entropy. It was true that my conception of the second place had been irreversibly altered by the sight of L's horrible mural, and could never go back to what it had been, even if every trace of paint were to be buried beneath layers of limewash. It would have been the easiest thing in the world to turn it back to look exactly as it had been before, yet in that process it would somehow have become fake. A kind of forgetting – a betrayal of the truth of memory – would have been enacted, and this is perhaps how we become artificial in our own lives, Jeffers, by our incessant habit of deliberate forgetting. I thought of how much Tony would hate the mural, especially the snake wound around the tree in the middle – snakes being the only thing Tony is frightened of. The painting of this snake suddenly seemed to represent an attack on Tony by L, an attempt to defeat him. Was Tony defeated? Was that why he had gone away? I remembered how L had stood and stroked my hair and said 'There, there' to me while I cried my sorrow out. The memory made me falter, and for a moment I stopped talking to Tony in my heart. I wasn't sure, in that moment, whether Tony had ever stroked my hair and said 'There, there,' nor whether he even could or was likely to do such a thing, and it seemed just then that it was the only thing I had ever wanted a man to do for me. This, in other words, wasn't L's attack on Tony – it was really *my* attack, made possible through L, who had enabled me to doubt him!

'Oh Tony,' I said to him in my heart, 'tell me what the truth is! Is it wrong to want things that you can't give me? Am I fooling myself into believing that it's right for us to be together, just because it's easier and nicer that way?'

For the first time, Jeffers, I considered the possibility that art – not just L's art but the whole notion of art – might itself be a serpent, whispering in our ears, sapping away all our satisfaction and our belief in the things of this world with the idea that there was something higher and better within us which could never be equalled by what was right in front of us. The distance of art suddenly felt like nothing but the distance in myself, the coldest, loneliest distance in the world from true love and belonging. Tony didn't believe in art – he believed in people, their goodness and their badness, and he believed in nature. He believed in me, and I believed in this infernal distance in myself and in all things, in which their reality could be transmuted.

Tony had told me, a few days before he left, about a strange encounter he had had with L in the glade. Tony had just shot a deer there, since deer were breaking in and eating the tree bark, which would cause the trees eventually to die. Tony was glad he had managed to cull this deer, which he intended to skin and prepare for us to eat. He was walking through the glade carrying the dead deer over his shoulders when he met L on the path, and far from congratulating Tony on his catch, L had become angry, even after Tony had given him his reasons for shooting the deer.

'I won't have killing done near me,' L apparently said, and he had gone on to say that as far as he was concerned the trees could fend for themselves.

He didn't seem to recognise that this was Tony's property and that Tony could do what he wanted here, and I believe the reason he didn't was because L's conception of property was as a set of inalienable rights attached to himself. His property was the radial sphere of his own persona; it was the environs of wherever he happened to be. He was defending his right not to be trespassed on by whoever might choose to come and let off a gun right next to his ear – or so I was able to surmise. What I said to Tony was that perhaps it was because L had grown up in a slaughterhouse and had an aversion to the deaths of animals.

'Maybe,' Tony said. 'All he said was that what I did was worse than what the deer had done. But I don't think so. There are some things you have to be able to kill.'

I thought about this story, while I sat on the bed and stared at the rain, and what I thought was that Tony and L were both right, but that Tony was right in a way that was sadder and harder and more permanent. Tony accepted reality and saw his place in it as something he was responsible for: L objected to reality and was always trying to free himself from its strictures, which meant that he believed himself responsible for nothing. And my own desire to be stroked and comforted and to have the bad things that had happened atoned for lay somewhere between the two, and that was the reason I had run away from Tony in the glade.

On the evening of the fifth day the door to my room opened and there on the threshold stood Tony, as large as life! We looked at each other, and both of us were remembering the last time we had looked at each other, Tony from the window and I from down below in the trees, and I saw that we each knew we had spent some part of ourselves in that moment that would never be restored to us, and that we were going to walk on in this humbler and more depleted condition.

'Did you hear me?' I said, holding my breath.

Slowly he nodded his big head, and then he held out his arms and I flew into them.

'Please forgive me!' I said. 'I know that what I did was wrong. I promise never to make you go away again!'

'I forgive you,' he said. 'I know you only made a mistake.'

'Where have you been?' I said. 'Where did you go?'

'To the cabin at North Hills,' he said, and I bowed my head sadly, because the cabin at North Hills is my favourite place in all the world, and is where Tony took me when we first fell in love.

'Oh,' I said. 'Was it very lovely?'

Tony was silent, and so I thought I would never know whether North Hills was still lovely if I wasn't there, and it seemed right that I shouldn't know, because I had hurt Tony and there was no point pretending that I hadn't, or hoping that things had been ruined for him as a result. But then he said, stating what ought to have been obvious to me:

'I came back.'

Well, we were very happy, and then we went downstairs and were happy some more, and Justine cooked a dinner for us, and even Kurt perked up a little at having Tony home with us again. North Hills is four or five hours' drive from the marsh, a lot of it on mud tracks, and it was late and I knew Tony must be tired, so when there was a knock at the door I told him just to go off to bed and went to answer it myself. There on the doorstep in the dark stood Brett, coatless and shivering and wild-eyed. I asked her what the matter was, and when she opened her mouth she shook so hard I could hear her teeth knocking together through the gash of her lips. She told me L was dead, or might be, she didn't know – he was lying on the bedroom floor and he wasn't moving, and she had been too frightened to go near him and check.

We all rushed up through the rain to the second place, and found L lying as Brett had described, except that now he was making great groans that showed at least he was alive, though they were the strangest and most terrible inhuman sounds I had ever heard. So Tony, after all his voyaging, got back in his truck and drove the two hours' distance to the hospital, with L on the back seat where we had packed him in with cushions and blankets, and Brett up front. He returned at dawn, with Brett but without L, who the doctors said had had a stroke.

They kept him there at the hospital for two weeks and then Tony and I drove to get him. He was very thin and frail, though he could walk, and he seemed in those two weeks to have become an old man – he was utterly crushed, Jeffers, and he walked with a sliding kind of step, and his bent legs and hunched-over shoulders made him look cowed, as though he had been frozen in the act of flinching. But it was his eyes that were most shocking, those lamp-like brilliant eyes that had seemed to cast revelation wherever they looked. They were blackened now, like two bombed-out rooms. The light in them was extinguished and they were filled with a horrifying darkness. The doctors spoke to us about his condition while L kept his head strangely alert, as though he were listening, but not to them. And this other-worldly attentiveness, while his ghoulish eyes seemed to stare at nothing, remained a characteristic of his new self, even once he was able to talk and move around freely. His physical recovery, in fact, was quite rapid, except for his right hand, of which he would never regain full use. It was very large and red and swollen, as though it were engorged with blood, and it hung horribly from his thin arm, lurid and inert.

We talked a lot, in that time – Tony and Justine and Brett and I – about what could or should happen, and when, and how. The first days of summer had come, full and warm, with big beneficent breezes blowing in from the marsh, but we barely noticed. We were a household of anxious ministers, pondering the strange disaster that had befallen us. There were countless phone calls and enquiries and practical investigations, and many, many discussions late into the night, but the end result of it all was that L stayed exactly where he was, in the second place, because there was nowhere else for him to go. He had no family and no home, and very little money, and although by then it had become easier for people to travel, we could find no one among his friends and associates prepared to accept responsibility for him. You know how fickle that world is, Jeffers, so there's no need for me to go into it here. In the end there was Brett and there was me, and while I acknowledged that these events had occurred on my soil, and that L had come here under my aegis, Brett struggled to see her own commitment to the situation as anything more than to a jolly escapade that had gone wrong. She had come along with L on a whim, not as a plan for life!

I often thought, Jeffers, during those days, of the importance of sustainability, and of how little we consider it in the decisions and actions we take. If we treated each moment as though it were a permanent condition, a place where we might find ourselves compelled to remain forever, how differently most of us would choose the things that moment contains! It may be that the happiest people are those who broadly adhere to this principle, who don't borrow against the moment, but instead invest it with what could acceptably continue into all moments without causing or receiving damage and destruction – but it requires a great deal of discipline and a degree of puritanical cold-heartedness to live in that way. I didn't blame Brett for her unwillingness to make a sacrifice of herself. It was evident by the second or third day after L's return from hospital that she had never taken care of anyone or anything in her life, and that she didn't intend to start now.

'I hope you don't think I'm a terrible scab,' she said, when she came to find me one afternoon to tell me that her cousin – the sea monster – was willing to fly up to get her and take her home.

I realised I didn't know where Brett's home actually was, and it turned out she didn't really have one – or rather, she had many, and therefore none at all. She lived in one or other of her father's houses around the world, and he would always give her a week or so's notice before he was due to arrive so that she had time to pack up and leave, because her stepmother didn't like to see her. Her father was a famous golfer – even I had heard of him, Jeffers – and very rich, and the one thing Brett had never learned to do was play golf, because her father had never taught her. So it goes, among our species! I hugged her while she cried a little, and said I thought it was exactly the right thing that she should go back to her life. Yet in my heart I knew that it was really only that she was running away from L and his misfortunes, and that for all her accomplishments and beauty she had no better grasp of life's meaning than to consider it for what did or didn't suit her. And what, in the end, was so wrong with that? It was Brett's privilege to run away, and by convincing myself it was also her misfortune I was probably just trying to cover up my envy of her. Abused as she was, she was nonetheless free – she didn't have to stay there and puzzle it out like the rest of us!

There was a dividend to her departure, however, which was that she offered to take Kurt with her. Her cousin was looking for a personal assistant, apparently, to manage his affairs for him, which seemed to consist mainly of flying around in his plane and living a life of idleness and wealth. Brett believed there were even some writing opportunities involved, since he was engaged in compiling a history of the family and probably needed some help with it.

'He's not terribly bright,' she said to Kurt, 'but he owns a lot of shares in a publishing house. He'd take very good care of you. He might even be able to get your novel published.'

Kurt seemed to accept all this as his due, and since L was so reduced, his self-assigned role as my protector had become somewhat obsolete. Even Justine admitted it was for the best, though she was a little scared, now that the prospect of separation was actually here. I told her she would always be able to find a white man to be obliterated by, if that was what she decided she wanted. When I said that she laughed, and much to my surprise said:

'Thank God you're my mother.'

And so, Jeffers, that chapter of our life at the marsh concluded, and another – much more opaque and uncertain – would have to begin. What did I feel, in that moment, about the drama I had provoked, as it moved into spheres that were beyond my control? I had never consciously thought that I could or would have to control L, and this had been my mistake, to underestimate my old adversary, fate. You see, I still somehow believed in the inexorability of that other force – the force of narrative, plot, call it what you will. I believed in the plot of life, and its assurance that all our actions will be assigned a meaning one way or another, and that things will turn out – no matter how long it takes – for the best. Quite how I had staggered along so far still holding on to this belief I didn't know. But I had, and if nothing else it was what had stopped me from just sitting down in the road and giving up long before this. That plotting part of me – another of the many names my will goes by – now stood directly counter to what L had summoned or awakened within me, or what in me had recognised him and thereby identified itself: the possibility of dissolution of identity itself, of release, with all of its cosmic, ungraspable meanings. Just as I was tiring of the sexual plot – the most distracting and misleading of all the plots – or it was tiring of me, along comes this new spiritual scheme for evading the unevadable, the destiny of the body! It was for L himself to represent it, to embody it – his was the body that had dissolved and given way, not mine. He had been frightened of me all along, and he had been right to be, because for all his talk of destroying me, I, it seemed, had destroyed him first. Though I didn't take it personally, Jeffers! What I think I represented to him was mortality, because I was a woman he couldn't obliterate or transfigure with his own desire. I was, in other words, his mother, the woman he had always feared would eat him and take away his form and life just as she had created it.

The image that remained in my mind through these tumultuous days was of Tony, on the night Brett came to tell us that L was lying on the floor of the second place. Once we had got there and taken a look at L and realised he needed to go to hospital, Tony had lifted L up into his arms and calmly carried him out of the bedroom. How L would have hated it, I thought, to see himself majestically carried by Tony like a broken doll! I had gone ahead of Tony into the main room to switch on the lights, and so I was watching him when he came through the doorway with L in his arms and saw for the first time the painting of Adam and Eve and the snake. He took it in, Jeffers, without hesitating or pausing, and it was as though he were walking unhesitatingly and calmly through a blazing fire from which he was rescuing the arsonist. I felt myself singed by that same fire in those moments: it flamed close to me, close enough to lick me with its hot tongue.

It is of course well known, Jeffers, that L's late work brought about the renaissance of his reputation and also earned him real fame, though I believe a part of that fame was simply owed to the voyeurism that always crops up around the aura of death. His self-portraits are veritable snapshots of death, aren't they? He met death the night of his stroke, and he lived with it – if not happily – ever after. Yet I personally still find too much of the iconography of self in those portraits, inevitably, I suppose. They harken back to the person he had been; they radiate obsession, and disbelief that this could happen – to him! But the self is our god – we have no other – and so these images met with great fascination and favour out in the world. And then there were the scientists, poring over this evidence of a neurological event, so beautifully and accurately described by L's brushstrokes. Those brushstrokes illuminated some of the mysteries that had taken place in the darkness of his brain. How useful an artist can be in the matter of representation! I have always believed that the truth of art is equal to any scientific truth, but it must retain the status of illusion. So I disliked L himself being used as proof of something and dragged, as it were, into the light. That light was indistinguishable at the time from the limelight, but it could just as easily become the light of cold-hearted scrutiny one day, and those same facts used as proof of something entirely different.

But it is the night paintings I want to talk about, and there the power of illusion is not surrendered. Those paintings were made at the marsh in a remarkably short period of time, and I want to say what I know of the conditions and process of their making.

After Brett had gone away and L was left alone at the second place, the question of how he should be cared for quickly arose. I knew that it would not be good for my relationship with Tony if I took on the role of L's nurse and was always at his beck and call: I had been to that precipice and looked over the edge, and nothing was going to drag me back there! Tony himself had to do a great deal for L in the early days, since his physical strength was required to lift him and move him around, and L was quite dependent on Tony for necessities, though he treated him with a high hand. He had returned from hospital with quite a peevish, fussy little manner, and also with a slight stutter, and one would hear him ordering Tony about like a veritable dauphin.

'T-t-t-tony, can you move the chair so it's f-facing the window? No, that's too c-c-close – further back – yes.'

I got used to the sight that had struck me so forcibly the first night I saw it, of Tony carrying L in his arms, sometimes all the way down to the bottom of the garden if there was something in the view L wanted to see. But as I have said, L recovered command of himself quite quickly, and Tony made him a pair of beautiful walking sticks out of sapling branches, and soon he could hobble around the place on his own. He was quite unable, however, to cook or care for himself, and when he began to work and needed to select and access his materials, it became clear someone would have to be on hand to assist him. Justine, to my surprise, volunteered for the role, and so Tony went back to his normal duties, and I found myself with just a little more to do than my usual nothing, looking after them both.

Does catastrophe have the power to free us, Jeffers? Can the intransigence of what we are be broken down by an attack violent enough to ensure we are only barely able to survive it? These were the questions I asked myself in the dawn of L's recovery, when a new and raw and formless energy began to emanate from him quite perceptibly. It was a jet of life spurting out of the great hole that had been blown through him, and it had no name and no knowledge and no direction of its own, and I watched him begin to grapple with it and try to take its measure. He made his first self-portrait three weeks after his return from hospital, and Justine described to me the agonies he went through, endeavouring to hold the brush in his deformed and swollen right hand. He preferred to paint standing up, she said, with a walking stick in his left hand and a mirror to the side of him. She held his palette for him, and selected and mixed the paints where he told her to. The movements of his arm were unspeakably slow and arduous, and he groaned continually, and was constantly dropping the brush because of the violent tremor in his hand. It can't have been very pleasant to assist him! That first picture, with its great diagonal sliding line of sight, the world pouring in at the top right corner and pouring out down at the bottom left, was shockingly crude – shocking because the accuracy of the moment could still be perceived through and behind it. It was mauled but still alive, in other words, and this dissonance between consciousness and physical being – and the horror of seeing it recorded, which was much like the horror of seeing a dying animal – became the signature characteristic of the self-portraits and the reason for their universal appeal, even when L was able to execute them with more control.

Soon, L was wanting to go outside, and Justine had the idea of hanging a toy horn she had found in her old toy box around his neck on a piece of string, so that he could squeeze the rubber balloon and honk it wherever he was if he needed her. I feared L would consider this an affront to his dignity, but in fact it seemed to delight and tickle him, and I was always hearing that faint honking sound coming from one place or another on the property, like the call of a bird as it makes its rounds in nature unseen. It was very useful, since he was starting to roam quite far, Justine said, and would sometimes find he couldn't get back, or would drop something and be unable to pick it up again. I could see that his destination was the marsh: he got a little closer to it every day. One afternoon I came upon him standing by the prow of the landlocked boat, just as he had been the day of our very first conversation, and this coincidence led me to exclaim, somewhat absurdly:

'So much has changed, and yet nothing has!'

When of course, Jeffers, it would have been as true – and as meaningless – to say that nothing had changed and yet so much had. One thing that hadn't changed was the repudiating, indifferent look that L so often bestowed on me and that I never, nonetheless, had got used to. Weak as he was, he bestowed it on me now, and said, falteringly:

'Y-you don't change. You never will. You won't let yourself.'

I was still public enemy number one, you see, even after all that had happened!

'I always try,' I said.

'Only a r-real emotion can change anyone. You'll be swept away,' he said, by which I understood him to mean that my unchangingness would be my doom, like the tree that breaks in the storm because it cannot bend.

'I have a protection,' I said to him, lifting my head.

'You have gone far but I have gone further,' he said, or I thought he said, for he spoke more indistinctly now than ever, 'and I know a destruction that passes over your protection.'

And this was more or less the tone of all my dealings with L from this point on. He was unfailingly hostile to me in the period of his recovery. It was as if the state of illness had offered him some ultimate opportunity for disinhibition. Another time he said to me:

'All the good in you has come out in your daughter. I wonder what is there now, where the good used to be.'

He got it into his head that I was always staring at him, and sometimes he would startle me by snapping the fingers of his left hand in front of my eyes.

'Look at you, staring at me like a hungry cat with your green eyes – well, I snap my fingers at you.'

Snap!

It all suddenly became too much for me, and one day when I was lacing my shoe I fainted and remember nothing of what happened for the next twenty-four hours – it seemed I was on holiday, lying on the bed with a smile on my face, while Tony and Justine took turns sitting anxiously beside me, holding my hand. When I got up, I discovered that a friend of L's had written to me asking whether he could come to visit. He was concerned about L, he said, whom he had known for many years, and even more concerned about me, and the predicament I had been put in by L's falling ill on my property. He also had some money from L's gallerist to give me, to set against whatever expenses I had run into on L's behalf. So I returned from my little sojourn in the underworld to find the world above was a bit saner than when I had left. I wrote back and said he could come when he liked – his name was Arthur – and a week or so later a car pulled up in the drive and there he was!

Arthur was a delight, Jeffers, a tall, handsome, debonair-looking fellow with a splendid shining mane of dark hair, who greatly surprised me once he had bounded out from his car and introduced himself by bursting into tears, something he was to do frequently over the course of his stay, whenever his sympathy and compassion were aroused.

He often kept talking and even smiling while he wept, as though it were a completely normal and natural phenomenon, like a rain shower. Tony was so amused by this habit that he would burst out laughing whenever Arthur did it.

'I'm not really laughing,' he would say to Arthur, his shoulders shaking with mirth. What he meant was that he wasn't laughing *at* him. 'It's just very nice.'

These two became very good friends and they are still close to this day, and call one another brother, so that it is almost as though Tony has regained the relative he lost in his youth. It makes me happy to attribute this gain in some way to L, from whose presence Tony had otherwise not profited. But sitting between them that first afternoon with one weeping and the other laughing, I did wonder what latest strange harbour my ship had weighed anchor in!

Arthur was keen to get across and see L, and while he was gone I made up a room for him in the main house. He came back a couple of hours later, his face aghast and his handsome hair standing on end in affront.

'It is quite shocking,' he said. 'You must not be expected to bear the responsibility.'

He had known L for more than twenty years, Jeffers, and probably knew more than anyone about his life. As a much younger man – he was now somewhere in his forties – Arthur had been L's studio assistant, when L was still successful enough to require such a thing. He had gone with L to openings, and watched him be touted around in front of collectors like an increasingly unmarriageable daughter, and realised he himself wanted nothing more to do with the art world, though he had hoped at one time to become a painter. Nonetheless he had stayed in touch with L through the years. It was true that L's circumstances were very much reduced, he said, as a lot of people's were in the light of recent events, but L's decline had been going on for a long time before that and he was now at the very bottom of the barrel of cash and goodwill. And he had no family he was prepared to recognise, but Arthur had managed to find a half sister of his who he thought might be persuaded to take him in. She still lived in the place where L had been born. His half brothers were all dead. If nothing else, the state there would have to take care of him, and Arthur was prepared to make the necessary arrangements.

Well, Jeffers, it was in one way a great relief to hear all this, but at the same time I couldn't bear the thought of L being consigned to the fate Arthur had described. If only he could have taken advantage of my goodwill, gotten along better with me, been nicer, kinder, more reciprocal . . .

'You can't expect to keep a snake as a pet,' Arthur said, sympathetically but accurately enough.

I was in turmoil nonetheless, believing somewhere inside me that if I could become capable of greater generosity, then L would be saved. But who or what did I think I was saving him from? I liked to think I was prepared to go to the ends of the earth for L – but only if he upheld his side of the bargain, and was grateful and polite and fitted in with the pleasant, comfortable vision of life I had offered him. Which he would and could never do!

'He isn't your responsibility,' Arthur repeated, seeing my distress, while the tears began to flow down his cheeks. 'He's a grown man who took his own chances. Believe me, he's always done exactly what he wanted and never given a thought to what anyone else felt about it. He's had the opposite life to someone like you – he hasn't inconvenienced himself for a minute on account of other people. Face it, he wouldn't help you,' he said kindly, wiping his eyes, 'if you were dying in front of him in the street.'

Despite everything, Jeffers, a part of me still believed that he would.

'By the way, have you seen what he's doing over there?' Arthur said. 'The self-portraits – they're just incredible.'

I have to say that worried as we were, we had a wonderful evening with Arthur, who was such fun, and when Justine came to join us and saw the handsome stranger she blushed to the roots of her hair and I saw how beautiful she had become, and that she was in a sense finished, and I wondered whether this was how a painter might feel, looking at a canvas and realising there was no more he could or ought to do to it. Arthur left the next morning, promising to be in touch very soon and to come back as soon as he could. And he did come back, but by then everything had changed again.

By the middle of the summer L was much more himself, though a shrunken and very irascible version. He wore a look now on his face that is difficult to describe, Jeffers – put simply, it was the look of a creature who has been caught by a bigger creature and knows there is now no possibility of escape. There was no resignation in it, and I don't suppose the creature feels terribly much resignation in the jaws of his captor either, despite the inexorability of his fate. No, it was more like the flash a bulb makes when the fuse gives out, illuminating and extinguishing in almost the same instant. L was caught in a long instant of illumination in which he realised, it seemed to me, his whole self and the extent of his being, because he was seeing at the same time the end of that being. In his expression, realisation and fear were indistinguishable from one another. Yet there was also a kind of wonder, as though at the original fact of his own existence.

It was around then that Justine began to say that L was sleeping much more during the day and working later at night. The weather was very warm, and there were often great bright moons, and she had started to find him sitting out by the prow of the boat long after darkness had fallen. In the morning she would discover him asleep on the couch in the main room, while numerous sketches lay scattered across the table. They were watercolour sketches, and all she could say was that they were pictures of darkness, and that they reminded her of how frightened she had been of the dark when she was a child and believed she could see things in it that weren't there.

One day, L asked her whether she couldn't find some bag or satchel for him to use so that he could take his materials outside with him, and she did find such a thing, and packed the materials he indicated into it. He had started to become very agitated, she said, at nightfall, and would move frantically around the room, sometimes knocking into the walls or upsetting the furniture, and though he was usually very kind and courteous to her he could some-times shout at her if she happened to call by when he was in that state. Hearing this, I decided Justine needed a night off. Since it was so warm, I suggested that Tony could take care of L for the evening, while she and I went down to one of the marsh creeks for a swim. One way or another we hadn't swum much that summer, though it was the thing I most liked to do. Usually we swam in the day – it had been years since I had done something so romantic as go down and swim in the moonlight! So after dinner Justine and I took our towels and left Tony to do the clear-ing up, and made our way down the garden and along the path to the marsh.

What a night it was, the moon so bright that it cast our shadows across the sandy earth, and so warm and wind-less that we could barely feel the air against our skin. The tide was in and the creeks were full and an opalescent sheen lay all across the water, and the moon burned its cold white path to our feet from the furthest horizon. And then, amid all this perfection, we realised that in our hurry we had forgotten to bring our swimming costumes!

The only thing for it was to swim naked, since neither of us wanted to go all the way back to the house, yet there was something taboo about this idea, at least for us, and I saw Justine hesitate as we realised our predicament. It is hard to understand, Jeffers, the physical awkwardness that grows up between a child and a parent, given the fleshli-ness of their bond. I had always been careful, once Justine was of an age to notice, not to impose my flesh on her, though it had taken me longer to accept her own need for privacy. I remember the surprise – almost the sadness – I felt, the first time she closed the door against me while she took her bath. How often I have been made to realise it is children who teach their parents, not the other way around! Perhaps this is not true of everyone, but speaking for myself I felt certain that of all bodies mine was the one Justine would least like to see unclothed, and I myself had not seen her naked for many years.

'We won't look,' I said to her in the end.

'All right,' she said.

And we flung off our clothes as fast as we could and ran shouting into the water. I believe there are certain moments in life that don't obey the laws of time and instead last forever, and this was one of them: I am living it still, Jeffers! We quickly grew quiet, after that initial boisterousness, and swam silently through water that in the moonlight seemed as thick and pale as milk and that left great smooth furrows behind us.

'Look!' Justine cried out. 'What's this?'

She had swum a little distance away from me and was floating and dipping her arms above and below the surface so that the water ran down them like molten light.

'It's phosphorescence,' I said, lifting up my own arms and watching the strange light flow weightlessly over them.

She cried out in wonder, for she had never seen this before, and it struck me, Jeffers, how the human capacity for receptivity is a kind of birthright, an asset given to us in the moment of our creation by which we are intended to regulate the currency of our souls. Unless we give back to life as much as we take from it, this faculty will fail us sooner or later. My difficulty, I saw then, had always lain in finding a way to give back all the impressions I had received, to render an account to a god who had never come and never come, despite my desire to surrender everything that was stored inside me. Yet even so my receptive faculty had not, for some reason, failed me: I had remained a devourer while yearning to become a creator, and I saw that I had summoned L across the continents intuitively believing that he could perform that transformative function for me, could release me into creative action. Well, he had obeyed, and apparently nothing significant had come of it, beyond the momentary flashes of insight between us that had been interspersed by so many hours of frustration and blankness and pain.

I swam to the end of the creek and when I turned around I saw Justine coming out of the water onto the sandbank. She was either unconscious of my looking or had decided not to notice it, for she stepped unhurriedly to get her towel, her white form revealed in the moonlight. She was so smooth and sturdy and unblemished, so new and strong! She stood as a deer stands, proudly with its antlers lifted, and there in the water I quailed before her power and her vulnerability, this creature I had made who seemed to be both of me and outside and beyond me. She dried herself quickly and dressed while I swam to the shore, and I was dressing too when she grabbed my arm and squeezed and said:

'Someone's there!'

We both looked into the long shadows beyond the path, and there indeed was a figure, sort of scurrying away.

'It's L,' Justine said wryly. 'Do you think he was watching us?'

Well, I didn't know whether he had been or not, but he certainly moved to get away faster than I might have expected him to! When we got back to the house we saw that far from looking after L, Tony had fallen asleep in his chair, and so I went across to the second place myself to make sure that all was well. There were no lights on, but the night was still so bright that I found my way easily through the glade, and as I approached could see quite clearly into the main room through the curtainless windows. Whether or not it was him we had seen on the marsh, L was now standing at his easel, and the moonlight fell in pale bands across him and across the furniture and the floor, so that he seemed almost to be a mere object among other objects. He was working in deep concentration, so deep that he barely moved, though I believe he was usually very kinetic and mobile in the act of painting. Nonetheless he was still, and watching him I realised that a certain kind of stillness is the most perfect form of action. He stood very close to the canvas, almost as though he were feeding from it, and therefore blocked my view of it. I stood there for a long time, not wanting to disturb him with any clumsy noise or movement, and then I very quietly went away, feeling that I had witnessed something in the way of a sacrament, the sort of sacrament that only occurs in nature, when an organism – be it the smallest flower or the largest beast – silently and unobserved confirms its own being.

I wish, Jeffers, I had paid more attention in the period

I am describing to you, not because I don't remember it, but because I didn't live it as I might have wished. If only something could tell us in advance which parts of life to pay attention to! We pay attention, for instance, when we're falling in love, and then afterwards as often as not we realise we were deluding ourselves. Those weeks in which L painted the night paintings were, for me, the opposite of falling in love. I went about in a low, almost mindless state, heaving myself out of bed in the morning and feeling as though I were carrying something dead inside me. The feeling constantly plagued me that I had been duped or tricked by life, and I remember being unable to stop a wry, fatalistic expression from creeping onto my face, which I would catch sight of sometimes in the mirror. I even stopped trying to communicate with Tony, which meant that our evenings were silent, because if I don't talk then no one will. Yet in those same days the very thing that I had wished for all along – that L would find a way of capturing the ineffability of the marsh land-scape, and thereby unlock and record something of my own soul – was occurring.

Justine told me that L was making a new painting every night, and that the same routine – the build-up of agitation over the course of a few hours, followed by him bursting out of the house with his bag of paints and plunging away into the dark – repeated itself each time. In other words, the paintings were produced almost as acts of performance, requiring this winding or working up of himself in advance, just as actors or other performers do. More than anything this should have told me that we were approaching an ending, since this extreme kind of behaviour was entirely unsustainable, but at the time all I felt was resentment at the labour and worry it was causing Justine. I did dimly perceive that L was travelling far outside himself in his nightly encounters, and that he must therefore have found something there that he went in pursuit of over and over again, but this only caused me to feel a vague suspicious kind of jealousy, the kind a wife feels when she suspects her husband of having an affair but won't yet admit it to herself. All I knew was that L had gone away from me, was not even considering me, while he exercised his entitlement to live in my environs, as if I didn't exist.

Then I met him unexpectedly one afternoon, when I was out trudging aimlessly along the marsh paths – he was sitting on one of the small bluffs that overlook the creeks. The marsh was quite dry by now from the heat, and its faded, fawn colours had an air of nostalgia to them, so that you seemed to be looking at it across a distance of time as well as space. There was the smell of sea lavender on the breezes that for me is the smell of summers, and even that scent seemed to hold a melancholy note, as though everything that had been and could ever be joyous and good lay irretrievably in the past. I think I would have walked past L, so exiled from him did I feel, had he not turned his head as I approached and – after a few seconds in which I am certain he did not recognise me – looked at me quite kindly.

'I'm glad you've come,' he said when I sat down next to him. 'We haven't always gotten along too well, have we?'

He spoke rather vaguely and distractedly, and though I was surprised by his remarks, I wondered at the same time whether he was quite conscious of what he was saying, and to whom.

'I don't know how to live my life any other way,' I said.

'It doesn't matter now,' he said, patting my hand in an avuncular kind of fashion. 'All that has gone. So many of our feelings are illusion,' he said.

How true, Jeffers, that observation felt to me!

'I have made a discovery,' he said.

'Will you tell me what it is?'

He turned his empty eyes on me, and the sight of those dead circles made an awful pain go through me. I didn't need to hear what his discovery was – I could see it right there!

'It's so lovely here,' he said after a while. 'I like watching the birds. They make me laugh, they enjoy being themselves so. We're awfully cruel to our bodies, you know. Then they refuse to live for us.'

I don't believe he was talking about death, but about the non-being in life that most of us go in for.

'You've always pleased yourself,' I said, somewhat bitterly, because it did seem to me that that was what he had done, and what most men did.

'But it turns out,' he said after a while, as though I hadn't spoken, 'that nothing is real after all.'

I think I understood then that his illness had released him from his own identity and history and memory so violently and thoroughly that he had been able at last to really see. And what he had seen was not death, but unreality. This, I believe, was the discovery he had made, and it was what the night paintings told of – and the question I wish

I had asked him that afternoon on the marsh was about what came after that discovery, but perhaps L didn't know the answer to that question any more than the rest of us do. Instead we sat there and watched the birds floating and hovering on the breezes, and after half an hour or more of sitting in silence I got up while he stayed where he was, and seemed inclined to remain. He looked up at me, though, and he gripped my hand suddenly with his own strong, dry, bony hand and he said, in the same vague impersonal way:

'I know you're going to feel better soon.'

And we said goodbye to one another, and I never saw L again.

Tony had brought in a big crop of fruit and vegetables from the garden, and for two days after that I was imprisoned inside in the kitchen from dawn to dusk, sweating in clouds of heat and blanching and canning and preserving, which was what I was doing the morning Justine burst in and told me that L had gone.

'How could he have gone?' I said.

'I don't know!' she cried, and she handed me a note.

M

I decided to move on. I'll try to get to Paris after all. Do what you want with the paintings, except for number seven. That one's for Justine. Be so kind as to give it to her.

L

So! Half-crippled as he was, he had set off in pursuit of that old sexual fantasy, and decided to throw his tattered hat in the ring of life once more! Well, Jeffers, there were all kinds of pandemonium while we tried to find out where he had got to and how, but in the end the mystery was solved simply enough when one of the men mentioned to Tony that he himself had driven L to the station, after L had accosted him in a field near the house a week or so earlier to ask the favour. They had arranged a time, and L had offered to pay and been politely refused, and the man had assumed it was all perfectly open and above board. Which in a way, I suppose, it was.

I have never been able to find out the precise details of L's journey and of how he managed to get so far out into the world from our tiny station in his weakened state, but it is well known that he died in Paris in a hotel room not long after he arrived, of another stroke. Soon after that news came, Arthur pulled up in our driveway again and together we went through everything, and packed up all the paintings and the sketches, and all L's notebooks and other materials, and one day a big van arrived to take it away to L's gallery in New York. It wasn't long before the rumble that started over there became audible here, and I began to get all kinds of enquiries and demands for information, and to see my name appearing in the articles that soon started to come out about L's last paintings. It turned out that he had corresponded with a number of people during his time in the second place, and had wasted no opportunity to tell them the most terrible and vituperative things about me and about the controlling, destructive kind of woman I was, and about Tony, whom he mentioned rather obsessively, always – and only just – stopping short of making fun of him and putting him down.

Tony was calm enough about it, given how much he had done for L and how little he had profited in the history of our dealings with him.

'Did you trust him?' I asked, since I believed he never had.

'Only a wild animal doesn't trust anybody,' Tony said.

He didn't care about the articles, since no one he knew ever read the kinds of papers these things were printed in, but he had observed how much L's opinions affected me and he worried my life with him at the marsh might now be spoiled.

'Do you want to go somewhere else?' he asked me, which in terms of a sacrifice was like him offering to sever his own right arm.

'Tony,' I said to him, '*you* are my life – you're my whole security in living. Where you are, the food I eat tastes better, I sleep better, and the things I see feel real, instead of like pale shadows!'

As for me, I have been disliked all my life, since I was the tiniest child, and have learned to live with it, because the few people I myself have liked have always liked me back – all except for L. His calumny, therefore, had a rare power over me. Hearing the dreadful things he had said about me, it seemed to me there was nothing stable, no actual truth in all the universe, save the immutable one, that nothing exists except what one creates for oneself. To realise this is to bid a last and lonely farewell to dreams.

More wrestling than dancing, Jeffers, as Nietzsche described living!

So I gave up L, gave him up in my heart, and filled in the secret place inside myself that I had kept free for him all along. Someone wrote to ask whether it was true there was a mural painted by L's hand on my property, and I went to town and bought a big tin of limewash, and Tony and I painted over Adam and Eve and the snake, and I rehung the curtains in the second place and told Justine she could consider it hers, and for her own use, whatever and whenever that might be.

She put her night painting – number seven – in there: as its owner, she now has the peculiar distinction of being the wealthiest person I know! Though I don't believe she will ever sell it. But I like to think that, however unwittingly, L gave her freedom, the freedom not to look to others for the means of her survival that is still so hard for a woman to come by. She is in love with Arthur, of course, so that game of chance is still hers to play – as, I suppose, it will always be. Might it be true that half of freedom is the willingness to take it when it's offered? That each of us as individuals must grasp this as a sacred duty, and also as the limit of what we can do for one another? It is hard for me to believe it, because injustice has always seemed so much stronger to me than any human soul. I lost my chance to be free, perhaps, when I became Justine's mother and decided to love her in the way that I do, because I will always fear for her and for what the unjust world might do to her.

The painting is rather the odd one out of the series, and to my mind the most mysterious and beautiful of all, since unlike the others it has two half-forms in it – amid all the extraordinary textures of darkness – that seem to be composed of light. They seem almost to be beseeching one another, or striving to unify, and in their striving the oneness miraculously occurs. I go in often to look at it, and I never tire of watching that tension between the two shapes resolve itself before my eyes. I like to think, fancifully of course, that this was what L saw, the night he glimpsed Justine and me swimming.

Several months after these events, a letter came for me with a Paris postmark. Inside it was another letter. The second letter was from L. The first letter was from someone called Paulette, who wrote that she had been trying to find an address for me, having recovered an unaddressed letter from the hotel room in which L had died, which she believed was intended for me. She had read the numerous articles about L and had decided that I must be the 'M' of the letter. She was sorry it had taken so long for her to get it to me.

I opened it, Jeffers, with hands that didn't tremble as much as you might expect. I believe I had – and have – come to see through the illusion of personal feeling, as L described it that day on the marsh. So many of the passionate feelings that have ruled me at one time or another have completely faded out of me. Why, then, should I let any feeling claim entitlement to lodge in my heart? I hope I have become, or am becoming, a clear channel. In my own way I think I have come to see something of what L saw at the end, and recorded in the night paintings. The truth lies not in any claim to reality, but in

179

the place where what is real moves beyond our interpretation of it. True art means seeking to capture the unreal. Do you think so, Jeffers?

M

Did you tell me it was a bad idea to come here? If you did then you were right. You were right about quite a few things, if it makes any difference. Some people like to be told that.

Well, the edge is here, and I have fallen over it. I'm in a hotel and it's cold and dirty. Candy's daughter was meant to be coming to get me but she hasn't come for three days now and I don't know when she will ever come.

I miss your place. Why are things more actual afterward than when they happen? I wish I had stayed, but at the time I wanted to go. I wish we could have lived together sympathetically. Now I can't see why we couldn't.

I'm sorry for what I cost you.

This is a bad place.

L

Second Place owes a debt to *Lorenzo in Taos*, Mabel Dodge Luhan's 1932 memoir of the time D. H. Lawrence came to stay with her in Taos, New Mexico. My version – in which the Lawrence figure is a painter, not a writer – is intended as a tribute to her spirit.

A NOTE ABOUT THE AUTHOR

Rachel Cusk is the author of the Outline trilogy, the memoirs *A Life's Work* and *Aftermath*, and several other works of fiction and nonfiction. She is a Guggenheim Fellow. She lives in Paris.